RAVES FOR HARRISON'S FIRST MYSTERY!

"Harrison makes his debut in an electrifyingly witty and suspenseful adventure that reads like the work of a seasoned pro . . . Crime fiction buffs will want more."
—**Publishers Weekly**

"The Victorian underworld comes alive, in all its richness and squalor, in this complex historical mystery . . . Historically vivid, fast moving, and fascinating."
—**Booklist**

"A first-rate debut . . . Unintrusive period detail, a large but vivid cast of characters, and grace and gusto in the stylish narration: a fine opener overall, especially for readers partial to gaslit English atmosphere."
—**Kirkus Reviews**

Why *Kill* Arthur Potter?

RAY HARRISON

POPULAR LIBRARY

An Imprint of Warner Books, Inc.

A Warner Communications Company

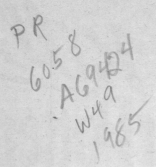

POPULAR LIBRARY EDITION

Published in Britain as *French Ordinary Murder*

Copyright © 1983 by Ray Harrison

This Popular Library Edition is published by arrangement with Charles Scribner's Sons

Popular Library books are published by
Warner Books, Inc.
75 Rockefeller Plaza
New York, N.Y. 10019

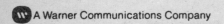 A Warner Communications Company

Printed in the United States of America

First Popular Library Printing: August, 1985

10 9 8 7 6 5 4 3 2 1

To my wife Gwyneth

Prologue

Arthur Potter slackened his pace. Now that it was over there was no need for hurry. He chuckled to himself as he thought of the tension of the last few days, somehow much worse than before. But the prize was greater this time, enough to change everything. He would have to leave, of course, but he'd known that all along. He should have gone really big the first time. There wasn't any point in nibbling — a big bite and off, that was the thing. And he would be off this time, for sure. He felt a growing elation, and laughed at the clerks scurrying home for a few hours — a meal, bed, then off for the train again. He'd been one of them, and now he was free of it!

He began to cross the street, then checked while a hansom clattered past. He took a few measured steps. Was he 'sauntering', he wondered, or 'ambling'? A few more steps. 'Sauntering' was better, it had a feeling of leisured purpose about it — just like the nobs. They didn't rush about, but they knew where they were going all right. Well, so did he! Tonight he'd joined the leisured classes — he was going to saunter through life from now on!

A policeman was standing in a doorway, the rime on his beard glistening in the gas-light. A moment of fear, an urge to hurry past. No, that would be stupid. Act naturally, relax, there was nothing to worry about.

'Good evening, constable,' he smiled.

'Good evening, sir.' The policeman brought his finger up to the rim of his helmet in salute.

Potter nearly laughed aloud. A bobby saluting him! If only he knew! All you needed was a bit of money and everybody looked up to you — and that was how it would be in the future . . . Still, he shouldn't have been so friendly with the bobby, he would have to be more careful. He glanced over his shoulder and fancied the policeman was looking after him. He would turn off up the next side street, lose himself in the crowd going to Fenchurch Street Station.

Once into the dimness he felt safer, in twenty yards he'd be lost in the fog. That was something else: he'd even be able to get away from the fog! Buy a new house in Tottenham and be finished with the City for good! He'd have to give in his notice. Old Smallshaw would be surprised – probably try to persuade him to stay! He thought of the stress of another week at the office. Better not go back at all – just write and say he'd left. They could keep their week's wages. If he'd thought it out properly he could have popped the letter in now, as he went past. He looked around him. The crowd had thinned, and through the greyness he could see the black outline of the viaduct towering over him. He would cut through French Ordinary – give himself a treat!

He wondered what Daisy would think, him not going to work anymore. He wished he could tell her, show how he'd bested them. But she'd only go all broody. No, it would have to be a win on the horses, a oncer, lucky first time. He should have found out about racing . . . Perhaps he should pretend to go to work for a bit, while he sorted things out.

He cursed as he bumped into a costermonger's barrow. Anyway, it would never work, she'd find out somehow. He listened with irritation to the footsteps overtaking him. It sounded like a group of workmen. Looking back he could see shapes outlined against the grey of the archway, indistinct and menacing. He was under the railway arch itself now; the footpath running along the left side. The gateway into Church Row, with its glimmering gas lamp, was fifty yards ahead. Should he dive over to the right among the barrows, and let them pass? But he couldn't escape that way . . . He took hold of his mounting fear. It was stupid to want to avoid them, they were probably just going home . . . but they'd hardly be going into the centre of the City, not working men.

They were close now, their boots scraping the cobbles . . .

He could hear their straining breath . . . Why weren't they talking? A sudden panic gripped him, and he started to run. There was a swift scrabble of feet and he felt his arms seized. He struggled and started to shout, pulling towards the distant light. He felt a fierce lance of pain from a blow in the kidneys, his legs drained of their strength. They were all round him now, shouting and laughing . . . His cries would never be heard! He wrested his right hand free and struck at the face of one of his assailants, then his wrist was caught and his arm twisted back. As his body arched against the pain he was punched viciously in the stomach . . . his strength was going . . . he couldn't get his breath . . . he felt himself vomiting in waves of pain.

He was aware of being dragged over the cobbles, hands tore open his coat and lugged at his pockets. Then he was dropped to the floor, while his attackers crowded to the corner to shelter the light of a small lantern. He tried to curl up, to lessen the spasms . . . if the pain eased he might be able to get away. He moved his leg experimentally, and heard a clatter as a box fell. They were round him again, hauling him to his feet.

'Where's the paper?'

He looked towards the hoarse cockney voice. 'What paper?' he croaked.

'The money paper.'

He shook his head, and a shower of blows fell on his face and body.

'Where is it?'

'I . . . don't know . . . what . . .'

Another blow caught him in the stomach and he began to retch helplessly.

'Where is it?'

He tried to speak, but his throat would not function.

'What do they call the damn thing, Bert?'

Dimly he felt he'd heard something important. The name . . . he must remember . . . His senses began to swim, he felt more blows, heard through a swirl of pain the word 'cheque' repeated endlessly.

Then it stopped. The numbness began to clear from his brain and pain flowed through his battered body. As if on a distant plane, he could hear them talking

'What do we do, then?'

'He don't seem to know what we're on about.'

'Sure we've got the right bloke?'

'Course I'm sure – his name's on this letter, ain't it?'

'I'll try him with my tickler.'

'Now, Lofty, we was only to rough him up a bit . . .'

'We haven't got the paper yet 'ave we?'

'No.'

'An' he's done me eye for me, ain't he? We'll try my tickler! Hold him up lads!'

He hardly felt the hands hoisting him up, his mind was becoming remote from his brusied body.

'Where's the cheque?'

His head was pulled back by the hair, and a face thrust close to his.

'Where's the money paper?'

Another spasm racked his body and a small jet of vomit came from his mouth. There was a roar of anger. He heard rather than felt the blow. A red curtain was before his eyes, which gently faded to black.

1

Detective-Sergeant Joseph Bragg of the City of London Police finished his report and added his signature with a flourish. He leaned his bulk back in his chair and sighed with satisfaction. A nice little case, that one, just the right mixture of routine and intuition. He disliked investigations which turned into a mechanical grind, they dragged police work down to the same level as the crimes themselves. No, there had to be an element of artistry in it, and the Peters case was a perfect example.

He leafed through his report again, tugging the end of his untidy moustache in concentration. Yes, it was just about right; a few nice touches to show up modestly the crucial deductions – should do his reputation a bit of good.

He rose and, crossing to the window, peered out at the traffic in Old Jewry below. A large closed van had become entangled with a coal lorry. Probably from a bonded warehouse on the river, full of port for Christmas. Its driver was shaking his whip furiously at the coalmen, who went on emptying their sacks with uncaring slowness. The blocked traffic stretched back as far as the main road. Bragg glanced across at the church and automatically checked his watch by the clock. It looked bad, a traffic jam in front of the police headquarters. The uniformed branch ought to manage things better than that.

There was a tap at the door.

'Come in!'

The young man who entered was dressed in a faultlessly cut vicuna frock-coat and immaculate grey checked trousers. He carried a silk top-hat and gloves, and from his right hand dangled a silver-topped cane.

'Sergeant Bragg?'

'Yes, sir, what can I do for you?'

'I'm Constable Morton. I was told to report to you this morning.'

'You're who?' exclaimed Bragg.

'Constable Morton. I've just been transferred from sixth division for plain-clothes duties.'

Bragg savoured the crushing reply he could make, and decided against it. 'Ah yes. Sit down, will you, lad? I'll be with you in a minute.'

He pretended to be deep in thought, while he covertly examined the newcomer from under his bushy eyebrows. A big man, of course, and the cut of his clothes showed off the lithe muscularity of his frame. An athlete clearly – maybe a boxer. Bragg warmed to the idea. His brown wavy hair was cut fashionably short and parted in the middle, his fresh face was clean shaven, he had a relaxed confident manner. All of which made him a distinct oddity.

'Right,' said Bragg crossing to his desk. 'We have a personal particulars form in the detective division. If we fill that in I shall know a good bit about you, and we can go on from there.' He took a blank form from his drawer and dipped his pen in the inkwell. 'Surname?'

'Morton.'

'Christian names?'

'James Eversleigh Kerwood.'

Bragg looked up sharply but Morton was totally composed. 'James what?'

'Eversleigh,' replied Morton, emphasizing the syllables.

'L – E – A?' asked Bragg.

'No, L – E – I – G – H.'

'And the last one was Kerwood?'

'Yes – like Kenwood with an R.'

'Who hung that lot on you?' asked Bragg, trying to cram them into the hopelessly inadequate space.

'One makes genuflexions in various directions, I suppose,' smiled Morton. The smile transformed his fashion-plate appearance. The wide mouth and white even teeth would be attractive to women – no doubt of that; and at the same time the open face projected a friendliness anyone would find difficult to resist.

'What do you mean by that?'

'Well, take Eversleigh. That was the married name of my father's eldest sister. Her husband was a banker, and they had no children. I imagine it was felt that the gesture might divert some of their money to me.'

'And did it?'

'By no means! My uncle drank himself to death, and my aunt spent most of his estate buying up ale houses and turning them into hostels for the deserving poor. The rest she's left to the Temperance Society.'

'Ah well,' said Bragg sardonically. 'It's only money . . . Age?'

'Twenty-four.'

'How long have you been on the force?'

'Since October 1888.'

'You've just done your two years on the beat then?'

'Yes.'

'Address?'

'One Alderman's Walk.'

'That's off Bishopsgate, isn't it?'

'Yes, between St Botolph's and the White Hart.'

'Ah yes. Lodge there, do you?'

'I have the rooms over the ground-floor shop.'

'You are the householder?' asked Bragg in perplexity.

'That's right.'

'Hmmm . . . Schools attended?'

'I didn't go to school as such.'

'You didn't go to school?' exclaimed Bragg incredulously.

'I had tutors at home.' This time the young man clearly felt the need to elaborate. 'My mother is a great admirer of Robert Lowe, and, as you know, he had no time for public schools. My parents quarrelled endlessly about education, and in the end they compromised. My elder brother went to Winchester and then into the army. I was educated privately.'

'I see . . . I'll put "privately" then?'

'I would think so.'

'The next is "Relevant examinations passed". You won't have anything to put there?'

'I don't suppose a degree is relevant?' asked Morton.

'How do you mean?'

'Well, I took a rather bad second at Cambridge – too much sport,' he added apologetically.

Bragg felt himself floundering. This one was totally outside his experience. Usually they were brightish lads taken off the beat, but with nothing better than elementary education. Only once had he been given a grammar school boy – he'd been too clever by half. Now this! He fought down a growing sense of outrage.

'Right, lad! The first thing is to get yourself dressed for the job. You said plain clothes, and plain clothes it is. It's no use walking around like a Piccadilly Johnnie. A detective has got to be inconspicuous, not stick out like a tart in a chapel.'

'Sorry, sergeant.'

'Go and get yourself some ordinary clothes, and a billy-cock hat. Try and make yourself look like a City clerk. And go to Goy's or Hyam's, not Savile Row.' Bragg noted with satisfaction that he had dented the young man's self-possession.

'Get back here as soon as you can . . . Oh, and if you need an advance on your plain-clothes allowance, I can lend you a couple of bob!'

Morton turned at the door and held Bragg's eyes for a moment, then he grinned broadly. 'I think I'll be able to manage, thank you, sergeant.'

'Well now, Constable Tait, where exactly did you find the body?' asked Bragg.

'Over there in the corner, where the arch is closed off by the wall of the warehouse.'

Bragg went over and dropped on one knee on the dusty cobbles. 'How was it lying?' he asked.

'Just all of a heap against the wall. I wouldn't have seen

it, only I noticed the barrows were all upturned and that. I came across and he kind of showed up in me lantern against the whitewashed wall. Thought it were a tramp at first.'

'What time was this?'

'Twenty to ten. I was finishing at ten, see, and I was working me way back to the station.'

Aye, thought Bragg, and intending to have a quiet smoke in the corner. 'What did you do then?' he asked.

'I ran to the station, being' as it was so close. Sergeant Johnson said to get him up to the mortuary straight away.'

Bragg kicked at a wooden crate in vexation. Really! The uniformed branch had the mentality of street sweepers!

'Footpads, you reckon?' he asked. .

'That's what it looked like, sergeant. He was fair knocked about.'

'I don't like it, constable. We haven't had any rampsmen in the City for ten years or more.'

'They can alway start again, I suppose.'

'But why now? Anywhere around there's easier pickings, with Christmas coming. Why rob some poor sodding clerk? Do we know anything about him?'

'I dunno, sergeant, I haven't been in to the station yet.'

'Well, thank you for coming in early, constable.'

'That's all right, sergeant. There is one other thing . . . I'm pretty sure I saw him earlier in the evening – about half seven.'

'Oh? Where?'

'I was walking up the west side of Minories, and he crossed the road towards me.'

'Are you sure?'

'I think so. He was acting a bit strange, smiling to himself, and he came over the road in a funny way – slow and deliberate like. A cab driver had to rein in hard, or he'd have run him down.'

'Drunk?'

'No, I don't think so . . . more kind of excited. He said goodnight to me as he passed, and I'd swear he was sober.'

'Anything else you remember?'

'No, I don't think so.'

'Right, if you do, let me know.'

'But why should I waste my time training somebody who won't last?' complained Bragg.

Inspector Cotton gave an indulgent smile. 'Why should you be so sure he won't last, Bragg? He's already lasted two years on the beat. What more do you want?'

'It stands to reason he won't. With his education I don't know what he's doing here in the first place.'

'Since when has education been a handicap?' asked Cotton mildly.

'You know full well not many grammar school lads have been any good. The more education they have, the less they want routine and discipline. Start taking on people with degrees and we shall be all froth and no beer. What has young Morton got in common with your cracksman or housebreaker? His mind won't begin to work the same way – as a detective he won't get past the start.'

'It will be up to you to see that he does.'

'Look, sir,' urged Bragg. 'He's spent all his life so far idling about – he didn't even go to school! Picking up an idea here, and an opinion there, all between games of tennis and tea on the lawn. Never done a day's work in his life. He just won't fit in! Can you see him working away for days, knocking on doors, asking the same stupid questions of the same stupid people? It would be like . . . like expecting a racehorse to pull a brewer's dray!'

'It's no use being prejudiced against the man,' said Cotton tartly. 'He's done two years on the beat, and that's good enough for me. I haven't got his personal file from sixth division, but I had a telephonic conversation with Inspector Davis last week, and he seemed perfectly satisfied with him. As to getting on with people, I'm told he plays cricket for Kent and the lads think the world of him.'

'I'm thinking about the efficiency of the division, sir. Have you met Morton yet?'

'Not yet.'

'He came into my room this morning dressed like Sunday in Hyde Park: pearl tie-pin, carnation – the lot. "Sahg'nt Breag?" he said – I thought he was equerry to the Prince of Wales at the very least! And that was his idea of plain clothes! I ask you! Made me feel a damned fool.'

'You'll get over it,' said Cotton with a laugh.

'But let's be serious! If he stays on the force he can reasonably expect to be made sergeant, if he's very good he might become an Inspector . . . ' Bragg maliciously watched Cotton preening himself. 'If he's lucky as well as good he could make Chief Inspector. What would he be earning then? If we said four hundred a year, it would be all. I wager he spends that sort of money on presents for his dollymops!'

'It's no use complaining to me, Bragg,' said Cotton with a knowing smirk. 'In fact it's no use complaining to anyone. I gather from the C.I. that Morton is a protégé of the Commissioner himself. Some pet project of his – I don't know what. Perhaps Sir William thinks the detective division needs a bit of brain power.'

Bragg snorted.

'If it's any consolation, Sir William particularly asked that he should be put with you.' Cotton shuffled his papers. 'Give him three months, and if he's a failure I'll back you up – but mind it's a fair trial. Now, what about that murder in French Ordinary?'

'The dead man has been identified by his brother-in-law. He was a clerk from Bethnal Green. I'm going to see the widow now. I'll take Morton with me.'

'Robbery?'

'It looks that way, though what he could have been carrying to make it worth killing him, I can't imagine.'

'Ah well, it's not likely to trouble us much. When you get back I want a word with you about your October progress report.'

It was a shabby two-storeyed house; the door opened straight on to the narrow street, the windows were framed

with limp curtains. Above the door was an arched fanlight
on which an inexpert hand had painted the house number.
Their knock was answered by a plump young woman. Her
face was white and strained. In a seeming daze she showed
them into a little parlour, sparsely furnished. In the room
behind they could hear children quarrelling. She seated
herself on the other side of the empty grate and cradled her
breasts protectively.

'Your husband worked in the City, I suppose?' asked
Bragg.

'Yes, he was a clerk with Cross Shipping Company in
Leadenhall Street.'

'How long has he worked there?'

'Since before we were married.'

'A long time then?'

'Over ten years.' She answered the questions mechani-
cally, seemingly without thought.

'What did he do there?'

'He used to keep the books.'

'Did he ever have to carry money, do you know?'

'I don't think so . . . I don't know.'

'French Ordinary Court isn't on his way from the office to
Liverpool Street Station. Have you any idea why he was
there?'

'No . . . I've heard him say he liked the smell around
there . . . ' The thought seemed to touch some memory, and
her mouth puckered with the effort of keeping back her
tears.

'What did he do when he wasn't working?' asked Bragg.
'Did he go down to the local?'

'Oh no!' she replied with some spirit. 'Arthur wasn't one
to waste his time like that. He wanted to get on and better
himself. He read a lot of books, and twice a week he went to
the Working Men's Club. He said they talked politics and
things . . . ' She was staring fixedly into the grate, her mind
far away. 'We were just getting on our feet . . . this summer
we had our first holiday . . . Southend, a whole week . . . the
children'll never get another now.'

'What will you do?' asked Morton softly.

'I don't know. We shan't be able to stay here . . . p'raps we'll go to his sister's for a bit . . . I don't know . . . '

Her lips were trembling, tears not far away. Bragg patted her shoulder gently, and the two men went quietly from the room.

'It makes me so bloody wild, this sort of thing,' burst out Bragg as they walked away.

'What do you mean?' asked Morton in surprise.

'The whole system is rotten! This poor sod gets done in and their whole world collapses. One minute they've got a future – a nice little house, some furniture of their own; the next there's nothing. She's got two or three children to bring up and the only way is to sponge on her relatives and hold out her hand for charity. It makes me sick!'

He kicked a stone furiously along the gutter. 'And what's more they accept it! They don't write letters to *The Times*, they don't badger their MPs to have the roads made safer, they don't complain when they're thrown out of their home . . . they just crawl into a hole, out of sight . . . And the smug people, the upright people, the people like you – yes, and me – throw them a few coins and feel uplifted at their truly Christian generosity. I ask you! And the likes of Daisy Potter are grateful for it, because it's something they've no right to expect. Grateful!'

'I tell you one thing,' he went on, tapping Morton's shoulder in emphasis. 'We're going to get the bastards who've done this . . . and see they're topped for it!'

2

'Potter? Why yes, I've still got him on the table. Like to come down?' The pathologist turned without waiting for an answer, and led the way down a cold stone-flagged corridor. Small beside the policemen, he had a round cherubic face and a sagging mouth. As he spoke he would screw up his eyes, so that he seemed to be enjoying a private joke.

'I don't think I've met your constable, have I?'

'No, sir. This is Constable Morton, just joined us from sixth division.'

Dr Burney stopped, wiped his hand on the blood-stained apron covering his striped velveteen waistcoat, and held it out. 'Happy to meet you,' he beamed.

Morton took it with a tinge of revulsion. 'Thank you, sir.'

'Sergeant Bragg always seems to get the interesting ones, and this is no exception.'

They entered a long room with a ridged glass roof supported on iron girders. A dozen or so grey slate slabs were ranged along each wall; four of them held white-swathed forms. Burney led them through a low doorway into a small whitewashed room.

'This is where it all happens!' he remarked genially.

There was a long wooden bench under the window, littered with instruments and jars. In the corner was a glazed white sink and next to it a cabinet containing books and bottles. In the middle of the room was another mortuary slab on which a man's body lay supine. Burney took up a probe and advanced on the corpse with relish. 'Forensically speaking, I find this one fascinating,' he said with a smile. 'I would estimate that death occurred between seven and eight o'clock last evening. You can see from the contusions on the face and torso that he had been the victim of a savage attack. There has been considerable bleeding from the nose – I expect we shall find it's been fractured.' He tweaked the nose vigorously. 'Yes, I thought so. But the point I want to make is that none of these blows was much more than superficial. Certainly not delivered with sufficient force to kill a healthy young man.'

'What did he die of then?' asked Bragg.

'Here, help me turn him over,' said Burney, his glance inviting Morton to share the jest.

Morton pulled on the right forearm and the body rolled towards him, the head following drunkenly. He glimpsed a red mass where the back of the head had been opened up like a rabbit on a butcher's slab. His head began to swim, and perspiration broke out on his forehead. He averted his eyes, and breathed deeply to keep the nausea at bay.

'This is the one that killed him' said Burney cheerfully. 'And it was meant to! That's the blow of a practised killer. See, it was aimed with very considerable force at the base of the skull, fracturing the occipital bone which was driven upwards and inwards. Very interesting that.'

Morton could visualize him poking about in the red plup with the greatest good humour.

'A neddy?' asked Bragg.

'It would be about the right size,' replied Burney. 'If your constable will assist I'll show you how I think the blow was delivered . . . Are you feeling all right, my boy?'

'Yes, I think so, sir.'

'Right, well just bend forwards . . . further . . . Here, support yourself on the bench . . . that's fine. The point of impact was along this line.' Morton shuddered as the point of the probe was drawn across his neck. 'And in my view the force necessary could only have been produced by striking downwards. So it follows that the dead man must have been in this position when he was struck.' Burney pulled Morton's head down and tapped his neck with the probe. 'Like this.'

'He would be off balance,' observed Bragg. 'Was he falling, do you think?'

'It's possible, but if he was falling away from the blow, as he would be, it would argue enormous force behind it. No, I think it more likely that he was held up while it was done.'

'Are you saying it was deliberate murder?'

'So it would seem.'

'Then why the other blows?' asked Bragg.

'Perhaps he put up some resistance,' said Burney, 'though from the look of the hands it wasn't much.'

'Do you think the other blows were just to make it look like a footpadding?'

'That would certainly be consistent.'

'Any sign of drugs?'

'Well, I haven't opened him up yet, so you'll have to wait. Any particular reason for asking?'

'A constable saw him just before it happened. Said he was acting strangely, seemed excited.'

Burney peered at the dead man's eyes, and gave a non-committal grunt. 'Well, I'll bear it in mind. You should have a full report by Friday, if I don't hit any snags . . . And get your constable to put his head between his legs for a bit.' he added jovially. 'He'll feel better then!'

'How does an underworld killing strike you?' asked Bragg when they were back in his room.

'It doesn't seem to chime with what Mrs. Potter told us,' replied Morton tentatively.

'That's true. Not that wives always know the truth about their husbands. Very often they only know one side – or choose to know only one.'

'There's the two night out a week,' suggested Morton. 'He might not have been down at the Working Men's Club.'

'You're right. Go down and check that tomorrow, will you? Mind you, it sounds too regular to cover up villainy – more like another woman. You feeling all right now?'

'I don't think I've ever spent a more disagreeable half-hour than in the mortuary just now,' said Morton with a grimace.

'Find it shocking, did you?'

'It wasn't so much seeing the body with the post-mortem

half done, though that was bad enough. It was the way he seemed to gloat over it, grinning away while he poked about inside the head – it was positively ghoulish!'

'He takes a bit of getting used to, does our Dr Burney. But it's not a person to him. You'll notice that he doesn't talk about "his hands" or "her face", it's always "the hands", "the face". It's as if it was a railway engine and he's trying to find out what made the machinery stop.'

'I suppose it was the smiling.'

'Oh, he'd smile if you told him his daughter had run off with a dustman; he's made that way; but as far as his job's concerned he's the top. If he says somebody died from such-and-such a cause, then that's it – there's no argument.'

'What about his views on the direction of the blow?'

'He'll be right, make no mistake. Though whether he's right about Potter being held up is another matter.'

There was silence in the room as Bragg began to fill his pipe, rubbing the tobacco lovingly between his palms. Morton let his gaze drift to the window, where the turrets of the church tower were outlined against the darkening November sky.

'It worries me, this does,' resumed Bragg. 'Ordinary footpads would have walloped him one or two to quieten him while they got away – they wouldn't have smashed him like that. Why kill him?'

'Has there got to be a reason?'

'No,' replied Bragg slowly. 'But people generally act to a pattern, and when they don't I want to know why. It may be nothing to do with Potter himself, but until I know I shan't be satisfied.'

'At first sight, it was just a robbery with violence that went too far,' observed Morton.

'I know,' replied Bragg, 'and Inspector Cotton would be happy to write it off as such. But I don't think it's as simple as that . . . There's got to be more to it than a casual assault, the killing doesn't make sense otherwise. I think tomorrow I'll introduce you to my old friend Foxy Jock, see if he can help.'

'I was hoping,' said Morton diffidently, 'that I might have tomorrow as leave.'

'Oh? Why's that, then?'

'The Prince of Wales is opening the new electric tube line to Stockwell. My father has two tickets, and since my mother doesn't want to go . . .'

'I didn't know you were part of the Marlborough House set,' said Bragg sarcastically.

'We're not, really,' replied Morton. 'But my father is Lord Lieutenant of Kent, and since the line goes south of the river, he's been invited *ex officio*.'

'Oh well,' conceded Bragg grudgingly, 'public affairs will have to wait on His Royal Highness's pleasure, I suppose. Now if your social life allows it, you might like to come with me to find out a bit about Potter's work.'

Cross Shipping Company occupied the ground floor of a newish stone building. The architect had striven to create an impression of solidity and prosperity. Grecian pillars flanked the doorway, and over the arched portal full-breasted nymphs foreshadowed the rewards of commercial success. The charms of the girl who answered their knock, if on a more human scale, were no less seductive.

'I'd like to see the office manager for a few moments, miss,' said Bragg.

'That will be Mr Smallshaw,' she said, smiling. 'Is he expecting you?'

'No. We are police officers. We would like to ask him a few questions concerning Mr Potter.'

Her face became grave. 'Just wait here a moment, and I'll see if he's free.'

Morton watched her narrow waist disappearing down the hall. 'Do you think we've just met the Bethnal Green Working Men's Club?' he asked with a grin.

'She could work my club any time!' replied Bragg. 'Not a bad place they have here. Look at all the mahogany! Must have cost a guinea or two.'

'Will you come this way, please?' She gave Morton a

subdued smile as she led the way to a large room at the back
of the building. It had a bare deal floor and bars at the
window. Several clerks were perched on high stools with
account books in front of them. They looked up in curiosity
as Bragg and Morton entered. At the window end of the
room a middle-aged man rose from a scratched oak desk.

'What can I do for you, gentlemen?' he asked in a thin,
anxious voice. He was short and slight, and his eyes, magni-
fied by thick lenses, gave him a look of timid surprise.

'Sergeant Bragg and Constable Morton,' said Bragg. 'We
understand that a Mr Arthur Potter used to work here.'

'Yes, shocking business,' said Smallshaw, clasping his
hands defensively.

'I'd like you to tell us what kind of a man he was.'

The concerned frown lifted from Smallshaw's brow. 'Yes,
of course.' He indicated two chairs and resumed his seat.
'Potter had been working here for eleven and a half years,'
he began. 'Generally I found him very competent – more
competent than many of the young men you get today.'

He shot a baleful look at the backs of the other clerks,
who were straining to hear what passed. 'He was a little
pushful at times, but what young man isn't these days? He
was always on top of his work, I will say that for him, never
late and hardly ever sick.'

'Altogether a model employee,' observed Bragg.

'I suppose that's so,' agreed Smallshaw.

'What was his job?'

'He kept the expense side of the ledger. In a shipping
company we have a great many expenses to keep track of.'

'Yes, I'm sure,' murmured Bragg. 'Did he ever have to
carry money – to the bank, for instance?'

'No, we seldom receive cash here. We have very few
passengers, and the cargo receipts are all by cheque. Mr
Richardson deals with that side of things.' He indicated a
burly young man who was writing painstakingly in the
ledger before him.

'Did you by any chance send him on an errand on Monday evening?'

'No,' said Smallshaw, wide-eyed.

'We can't understand why he was found in French Ordinary. You would expect him to walk straight up to Liverpool Street.'

Smallshaw's owlish gaze was fixed on Bragg's face, but he ventured no opinion.

'Do you know if he had any private reason for going down in that direction?'

'We don't become involved with our employees on a personal basis,' Smallshaw replied sharply. 'It can cause too many problems.'

'I see. What was he paid?'

'A hundred pounds a year.'

'Not princely.'

'It was what he was worth.'

'Paid weekly?'

'Yes.'

'Do you know anything at all about his private life?' asked Bragg.

'Only that he was married, and had children.'

'You'll be seeing the widow is all right, I suppose?'

'That will be up to Sir Charles,' replied Smallshaw primly.

'I see. Do you mind if we have a quick look at Mr Potter's work?'

'Well . . . I'm not sure.' Smallshaw hesitated. ' Sir Charles isn't in this afternoon . . .'

'It would well be of assistance to us in finding his murderers,' said Bragg quietly.

'Yes . . . I'm sure Sir Charles won't mind,' decided Smallshaw, but the worried frown was back. 'If it's all right, I'll put you in a room on your own, where you won't be disturbed.'

'I really don't have any idea what I'm supposed to be looking for!' exclaimed Morton in desperation.

'Don't let it worry you,' replied Bragg with a laugh. 'I

have the advantage of having worked during my misspent youth in a shipping office in St Mary Axe.'

'Did you really?' asked Morton.

Bragg had his pipe going well now, and his head was surrounded by a blue haze. 'Young lad, green from the country . . . never had so much money in my life before. All of fifty-five quid a year it was, and I could have the time of my life!'

'What part of the country do you come from?' asked Morton.

'A little village near Dorchester called Turners Puddle,' replied Bragg. 'In my grandfather's time it was Turners Piddle, after the river, but that sounded too coarse for the last generation, so they changed it.' He puffed his pipe in silence for a while, then caught Morton watching him.

'A marvellous place to grow up,' he sighed. 'My father had a small carter's business – three or four waggons and a van. My first memory is being perched on the back of a big cart-horse, looking down at my father's grinning face, my mother all worried with her hand at her mouth . . . It seems like I grew up with horses. When I was a child they would pop me in the manger while they curry-combed them. I'd stand there peeping through the bars, and the horse would be nuzzling for hay, never once minding that I was keeping it back.'

'Did you go to work in the business?' asked Morton.

'Try to keep me out of it!' laughed Bragg. 'At nine I'd finished with school, and was mucking out the horses with the best of them. At eleven I was driving one of the small waggons. For all that I was a big strapping lad, I reckon my old dad took a bit of a chance there. Mind you, it saved him one lot of wages . . . Looking back, it was a hard breaking-in. Up at five in the morning, feed and water the horse, then walk to Dorchester with a load of hay – all of ten miles before breakfast. The roads were rutted and muddy, and sometimes in the winter you'd find a tree had blown down and was blocking the road. You'd wedge the wheels, then stand talking to the horse like a loony till it was light enough to fetch a woodman to clear the way . . . Best times were when I was sent to Poole for a load of softwood from the docks. I'd be up at a summer's daybreak, the dew sparkling on the hedgerow, and mist in the hollows. I would be at the docks by nine easy. I'd leave the cart to be loaded and stable old Bonny, and I'd be off round the docks peering into everything; watching the ships docking and unloading . . . fishing boats, coalers, tramps – the lot! And sometimes out to sea I'd catch a glimpse of a warship steaming to Portland Harbour. The bustle fascinated me, and the seamen with their foreign lingo and strange ways. To sit in the corner of a café and just watch the different ways they ate was an education. After Turners Puddle it seemed a great cosmopolitian city – sleepy little Poole! Funny how your perspective changes, isn't it? When I was fourteen I persuaded my father to let me take a job in a shipping office in Weymouth. There was I, barely scraping by in the three Rs, suddenly confronted with bills of lading, invoices, manifests, account books. That was a bit of a facer, too. But it was so interesting I couldn't help buckling down to learn what it was all about.'

'What made you come to London?' asked Morton.

'Ah, that's another story. Come on, we've got to get through these books tonight.'

'All right,' sighed Morton. 'What is it you want me to look for?'

'Just tell me if you see anything odd. The ledger you've got has the accounts with suppliers in it. See, this is the account with a firm of stationers. On the right side of the page you see the goods they've supplied, and on the left the payments to them by Cross Shipping. Ignore the totals. If there's anything wrong it'll be in the entries themselves.'

'Very well,' said Morton resignedly.

'I'm looking at a book with all the expenses in it, only put down day by day as they happened. That way I should get a good idea of the pattern of the business.'

There was silence in the room for a time, the slow turning

of pages punctuated by the scrape of a match and the creaking of Morton's chair.

'Was last year a leap year?' asked Morton suddenly.

'I don't know,' retorted Bragg. 'Work it out for yourself. Fours into eighteen go four, fours into twenty-eight go seven, fours . . . no, it wasn't.'

'Then there's something a bit odd here, because they've recorded a purchase on the twenty-ninth of February last year.'

Bragg crossed to Morton's table.

'See,' explained Morton, 'this is a ship's chandlers' account, with lots of entries in it. Near the bottom of this left-hand page you get "29th" in the date column, with ditto marks under it, then at the top of the right-hand page you get "1st March".'

'Let's pick it up from the year end,' suggested Bragg, turning back through the account. 'Here's the first of October . . . November . . . December . . .' he called, flicking over the pages. 'January . . . January it is. That's the twenty-ninth of January, so it looks as if there's something missing. We can soon check,' he cried, striding over to his own table. 'This book will show if there were any purchases in that period. What was the name of the chandlers?'

'Crowe and Scrutton, West India Dock Road.'

'Let's try February 1889,' he muttered as he ran his finger down the page. 'Here we are! Second of February, an anchor and twelve cork fenders. So it looks as if there's a page missing. Get that miserable bugger Smallshaw in and we'll see what he has to say!'

Morton went down to the reception area, where the young woman sat demurely at her desk.

She returned his smile with a flash of white teeth. 'Is there anything I can do for you?' she asked.

'I'm sure there are scores of things,' he grinned, 'but at the moment I'd just like to see Mr Smallshaw.'

With a toss of the head she was gone, and Morton went back to savour the triumph of his discovery.

'Mr Smallshaw,' said Bragg in a stern voice, 'there seems to be something wrong here. I wonder if you can help us.'

Smallshaw flushed, and his face took on a hunted look. 'I'm extremely sorry,' he bleated. 'I don't know how that can have happened.'

'That's all right, sir,' said Bragg, 'I'm sure you'll be able to put it right.'

'I'll do everything I can, of course,' replied Smallshaw clasping his hands.

'There seems to be a page missing from the account of Crowe and Scrutton.'

Smallshaw took the ledger and turned the pages with a practised hand. 'Oh dear, oh dear,' he muttered, 'yes, I see. I can't think how that can have happened.'

'You weren't aware of any missing pages in this ledger then?'

Bragg's question was altogether too aggressive for Smallshaw, and he merely shook his head.

'We've checked across to the Day Book, of course.'

'Of course . . . ' echoed Smallshaw.

'And we're satisfied there were transactions in February last year.'

'Yes, there would be,' said Smallshaw defensively. 'It's a very busy account.'

'I wonder if you can reconstruct the missing page for me from the Day Book and the Cash Book?'

'Of course. I'll do it myself.'

'Good! The day after tomorrow?'

'I'll get it done tonight.'

'Well, let's say first thing Monday morning, to be sure.'

'All right.'

'We'll be off then. Goodnight, sir.'

'Goodnight . . . er . . . Goodnight.'

3

'How was the new tube then?' asked Bragg.

Their hansom was trotting past Aldgate pump, its obelisk dwarfed by the gas lamp squatting on top.

'Quite amazing,' replied Morton, 'and really a little odd. There's no smoke, of course, which is marvellous. And it's so quiet. But there's nothing to see. The carriages don't even have proper windows, the walls are padded nearly to the roof, and you just sit there. When the train stops you can't tell whether you're at a station or not until they shout "Oval" or whatever.'

'I don't know that I'd be happy so far under the ground,' remarked Bragg. 'They'll be turning us all into moles next. I gather from the *Star* that His Royal Highness was his usual expansive self.'

'So he seemed,' agreed Morton.

'I don't know how they'll make that line pay,' pronounced Bragg. 'There'll be hundreds flocking to the City at eight o'clock in the morning, and going back at seven at night. But apart from that nothing.' He glanced across at Morton. 'Unless you count empty-headed people going to the cricket. No, I'm glad there's none of my money in it.'

'What do you invest in, sergeant?' asked Morton, straightfaced.

Bragg shot him a reproving look from under his eyebrows. 'Figure of speech, my lad, as you must bloody well know! Don't roast your sergeant, that's today's first lesson, and mind you learn it.'

'Sorry, sergeant.'

'No, lad,' went on Bragg, relenting, 'I invest in my belly, and I fear it's beginning to show. Well now, while you were disporting yourself with the idle rich, I was down in Bethnal

Green checking on our friend Potter. He used to go to the Working Men's Club all right – sounds a real Samuel Smiles, all self-improvement and flat ale! That club would bear watching too. From what I can see it's one of the muddier springs of Socialism – Fabian lectures, Atheism, the lot, with the *Workman's Times* in the lobby, and a pie and a pint in the basement . . .'

The cab suddenly rattled on to granite setts and Bragg heaved himself round to open the trap-door in the roof. 'Left at the White Hart,' he roared.

The cabby had got one wheel in a tramline, and was blaspheming vigorously. They tacked jerkily to the right, into the path of a hay cart, then swooped leftwards under a low archway into a street lined with dejected clapboard houses. Here they were immediately surrounded by ragged yelling children, running beside them and trying to clamber on to the steps. The cabby swore at them, and flicked his horse into a trot. It seemed to Morton that at any moment a bare foot must be crushed beneath the wheels as they swayed perilously down the narrow street. Then the urchins tired of the chase, and, flinging obscenities after them, retired to the shelter of the archway.

On the left the slums had been cleared to build a new Board School, which dominated the surrounding dwellings like a fortress. On the right was a red-brick factory and the imposing new building of the District Board of Works.

'Stop at the next corner,' called Bragg. 'There you are, my boy, Foxy Jock's jerryshop! Right in the Ripper country you are here.'

Three balls hung crookedly from the corner of the building; they were so encrusted with dirt that no trace of brass gleamed through. The paint was peeling from the windows, and the panes were so filthy that it was impossible to make out more than the outlines of the articles displayed. Bragg paid off the cab, and led the way into the shop. At the jangle of the bell a face peered suspiciously from a curtained alcove behind the scarred counter. A fringe of yellowish-white hair surrounded a grimy bald head. The flaccid face was a mottled pink, threaded with purple veins converging on the nose. A pair of rheumy eyes regarded them.

'Why, Sergeant Bragg!' cried a hoarse Scotch voice. 'How nice to see you!'

'You're a lying bastard, Jock,' said Bragg roughly, turning to Morton. 'Jock there is the biggest fence between Aldgate and Poplar – take a good look at him!'

'It's not true, sergeant,' cried Jock. 'It's simply not true!'

'Don't be taken in by the squalor,' went on Bragg, disregarding him. 'He lives in a villa on Hampstead Heath, with a carriage and pair. And every summer he takes the waters at Baden, and plays cards with the Prince of Wales.'

'Don't listen to him,' wailed Jock.

'If there's any villainy around here, you can be sure he's at the back of it. He's the putter-up behind half the unsolved robberies in the City.'

'I've never broken the law in my life!'

'What about the Portman ruby?' demanded Bragg, turning on him. 'Weren't we hunting that for weeks, and all the time it was in your safe?'

'It had been pledged,' howled Jock. 'It was in the book!'

'Some pledge!' snorted Bragg. 'What's the news of the Peters diamond?'

'Which one is that?'

'Come on,' cried Bragg harshly. 'Stop playing bloody games with me! The twenty-five-carat stone prigged from Peters last month!'

Jock passed a furtive tongue over his lips. 'Amsterdam,' he said.

'Amsterdam?'

'So they say.'

'Who says?' demanded Bragg fiercely.

Jock hesitated. 'They say . . .' he repeated.

Bragg scowled, and Jock flinched back. 'What are *they* saying about the murder in French Ordinary the other night?'

'How would I know about that, sergeant?'

'It was robbery, wasn't it?'

Jock remained mute.

'Who did it?' demanded Bragg.

'They say it was a gang from Millwall,' muttered Jock.

'Names, man, names!'

'The whisper is that Joe Ramshorn's suddenly flush with money.'

'Right, keep listening.'

'So your brother's in the army?'

Bragg and Morton were strolling past warehouses and grimy factories, along rutted streets congested with carts and scurrying men, towards the coroner's court in Golden Lane.

'He used to be till he was wounded,' replied Morton.

'Wounded? That's bad. How did it happen?'

'A Gilbert and Sullivan operation in the Sudan,' said Morton. 'They were going to relieve General Gordon in Khartoum. My brother was with the Guards Camel Regiment.'

'Camel Regiment? I don't believe it!'

'I told you it was grotesque! The whole campaign was straight out of a burlesque. The army even engaged Thomas Cook to transport the expedition up the Nile. They did! It's perfectly true! His paddle-steamers towed the boats up as far as the Second Cataract, with the men lying around smoking and playing cards. It was a real Cook's Tour. Then when they got to Korti they had to spend weeks waiting while the Camel Regiment learned to ride its camels.'

'That I would have liked to see,' said Bragg with a laugh.

'Then they marched off towards Khartoum in a great square, with the camels walking in the middle. In the end I don't think the camels were ever used in action at all. A Dervish army under Osman Digna followed them, and there was a skirmish or two, but the Dervishes always ran off. Then one morning,' went on Morton, the laughter fading from his voice, 'they topped a ridge and saw the Nile once more in the distance – and the Dervish army in front of it. General Stewart inspected the enemy, handed his telescope to his aide and said "Well, gentlemen, I think we'll have breakfast first." And they did! In full view of the enemy, with bullets spattering about them like the first drops of a thunderstorm, they solemnly got out the white tablecloths and sat down to breakfast! In the course of this preposterous charade, a bullet struck my brother in the spine.'

Bragg sucked in his breath sympathetically. 'Lucky it didn't kill him,' he said.

'It almost did. He was brought by camel and boat down to Alexandria, where they got the bullet out, and there he stayed. He wasn't well enough to come back to England until last year.'

'And what is he doing now?' asked Bragg.

'Nothing. He's paralysed from the waist down, and his wound has never really healed.'

'Good God! And all for Queen and Country, eh?' observed Bragg gruffly. 'Typical! The merchant princes of London, howling for more colonies, don't have to pay the price themselves. They grow fat at the expense of fools and idiots! . . . Ah, here we are.'

They ascended a flight of worn stone steps, and entered a gloomy corridor with a dark brown dado and a row of wooden chairs along one wall. A helmetless constable lounged by a doorway opposite.

'Potter case down first, is it, constable?' asked Bragg.

'S'right,' answered the man, tugging at a hangnail, then sucking his finger.

'For Christ's sake, stand up!' cried Bragg in irritation. 'You look more like a sack of shit than a policeman!'

The constable sprang to attention. 'Yes, sir,' he muttered.

'Sergeant Bragg, detective division, witness in the Potter case. Has the coroner turned up yet?'

'Yes, sergeant, he's just come.'

'That's better!' Bragg turned to Morton. 'Right, lad, let's go in and get a seat in the stalls.'

They took their places on a pew-like bench at the back of the court. Morton looked about him with interest. The coroner's desk was on a high dais, with the City's coat of arms resplendent in scarlet and gold behind it. To the left the coroner's officer was swearing in the jury. To the right was evidently the witness-box. For a moment Morton expected to see Potter's body neatly laid out on a slab in the well of the court.

The clerk rapped on his desk to call those present to order, his gabble drowned by the shuffle of boots as they stood. The coroner entered from a side door, and, having bowed to the court, took his seat. He was a small man, who had to lean forwards to see over the edge of his desk. He was wearing a black gown and a grubby white wig which merged with his long grey whiskers. A pair of half-spectacles was balanced on a hooked nose, and, when he peered about him on his short stiff neck, he resembled a barn owl seeking prey.

'Well now,' he called sharply as the shuffling subsided, 'the first case is Arthur Potter, seventeen Barnsley Street, Bethnal Green.' He had a light creaking voice, which turned every statement into a complaint. 'Can we have the evidence of identification?'

'Call Harold Webster!' cried the clerk.

'Call 'arold Webster,' echoed the constable outside.

A man of about thirty-five paused at the half-open door, then crossed with hesitant steps to the witness-box. He took the oath in a strained cockney voice, gripping the edge of the box with both hands.

'You are Harold Webster?' asked the coroner.

'Yes, mi lawd,'

'And you live at forty-six Headlam Street, Bethnal Green?'

'Yes, mi lawd.'

'You needn't call me "my lord",' observed the coroner with an indulgent twist of the lips: ' "your honour" will suffice.'

'Yes, sir.'

'What is your occupation, Mr Webster?'

'I'm a clerk in the goods office at Bethnal Green Station, your honour.'

'Very good. How long have you known the deceased, Arthur Potter?'

'About twelve years.'

'Did you know him well?'

'He was my brother-in-law.'

'Any have you seen the body of a man in the City of London mortuary?'

'Yes, mi lawd.'

'Do you identify it as the body of your brother-in-law, Arthur Potter?'

'Yes, your honour.'

'You have no doubt about it?'

'No.'

'Very well, you may go down now.'

A self-conscious smile of triumph flitted across Webster's face as he scuttled to a seat at the back of the court.

The coroner finished writing and looked up. 'We'll take the police evidence now,' he said.

Constable Tait, helmet in hand, walked heavily to the witness-box, and took the oath. 'PC 917 Tait,' he announced, as he produced his notebook from his breast pocket.

'Carry on, constable,' directed the coroner, dipping his pen in the inkwell.

'On the evening of Monday the first of November, at about nine-thirty o'clock, I was patrolling down French Ordinary Court –'

'Where's that?' interrupted the coroner.

'It's a little alley leading from Fenchurch Street to Crutched Friars, your honour. At the top end it's called Church Row, at the bottom end it's French Ordinary Court.'

'That would be in Aldgate Ward, wouldn't it?'

'Yes, your honour.'

'Very well.'

Tait consulted his notebook again. 'It was a very foggy night, and I was examining some costermongers' barrows under the railway arch –'

'Which arch is that, constable?' asked the coroner.

'Well, your honour, the railway lines to Fenchurch Street Station are up in the air just there, built on big arches. They're right behind the warehouses on that side of Crutched Friars. You get into the court through a gateway in the buildings – only there isn't no gate on it. When you come out of that you're under the railway arch.'

'I see, and costermongers have the habit of leaving their barrows there at night?'

'Yes, your honour.'

'Very well.'

Tait glanced down at his book. 'I was examining the barrows, when my lantern lit on the body of a man lying in the corner.'

'Among the barrows? . . . behind the barrows?' prompted the coroner.

'Behind the barrows . . . and at the side . . .'

'Which?' demanded the coroner with a frown.

'Well . . . the barrows were at the front, but when I went behind them I saw the body . . . lying at the back . . . only away from them.'

'Oh well,' sighed the coroner in resignation. 'How was it lying?'

'Sort of on its side, your honour. I thought at first it was a man in a state of inebriation, or a vagrant asleep. It was only when I shook him that I found he was dead.'

'Who certified death?' asked the coroner.

'Nobody, your honour. He were dead all right, he was cold when I found him.'

The coroner swivelled his head round sharply, and gave Tait a startled look. 'How long does it take you to patrol your beat, constable?' he asked.

'Twenty minutes, your honour.'

'And so you had been down French Ordinary Court every twenty minutes since . . . since when?'

'I came on duty at six o'clock, your honour.'

'And when you found him at thirty minutes after nine, you say he was already cold?'

'Well, cool-like,' muttered Tait uncomfortably.

'What's that? Speak up!' rapped out the coroner.

'He was very cool to the touch, your honour, cool enough to tell me he was dead.'

'But you didn't feel it incumbent upon you to summon a doctor to confirm that life was extinct?'

'No, sir, I ran for assistance to Mincing Lane Police Station, where I reported to the duty sergeant.'

'What happened then?'

'I was ordered to place the body on one of the barrows and convey it to the mortuary.'

'To the mortuary?' cried the coroner in amazement.

'Yes, your honour.'

'On a costermonger's barrow?'

'Yes.'

'You took it right across the City like that?'

'We put some blankets over it, of course, your honour.'

The coroner put down his pen and, leaning sideways, peered coldly at Tait over his spectacles. 'But you took the body away, without anyone in authority having seen it!'

Tait's face reddened. 'Well . . . I'd made my report to the duty sergeant . . .' he mumbled.

'Ah, yes, constable,' the coroner's voice took on a sarcastic edge. 'I mean without anyone in authority other than yourself having seen it.'

'Well, Constable Welch helped me load it on the barrow . . .'

'Why did you not inform the Beadle of the Ward, as is your duty?' demanded the coroner.

'I think the sergeant sent a message, only he was out.'

'And you called neither a doctor nor the officers of the detective division?'

'The sergeant said to get it up to the mortuary . . . if it was dead . . .'

The coroner swung round and fixed the foreman of the jury with his glance. 'Have you any questions for this witness?' he asked.

There was a hurried consultation. 'No, your honour.'

Tait left the box to a murmur of conversation.

'Someone's going to cop it, after this,' remarked Bragg in an undertone. 'I hope it isn't going to be me!'

'Who carried out the post-mortem?' the coroner asked his clerk.

'Dr Burney, your honour. Call Dr Burney!'

'Call Dr Burney!' came the echo from the corridor.

Burney hurried in, beaming from side to side like a caricature of royalty. He took the oath, and stood composedly in the witness-box.

'Dr Burney,' said the coroner, 'it appears that you were probably the first medical man to see the deceased after death. When did you first examine the corpse?'

'At twenty minutes after eight on the morning of Tuesday the second of November. From the condition of the body I judged that death had occurred some twelve to fourteen hours earlier.'

'Have you had reason to revise that opinion subsequently?'

'No, your honour. The contents of the stomach were examined in the laboratory, and the indication was that a light meal had been ingested some six hours earlier – cheese, sausage, pickled gherkin and beer,' he added with gusto.

'Have you been able to establish the cause of death?' asked the coroner.

'Yes, your honour, beyond all peradventure. There were extensive lacerations and contusions on the torso, which would be consistent with his having been assaulted by a number of people. But these were superficial. Death was caused by a single blow struck with prodigious force at the base of the skull. This fractured the occipital bone, and crushed the *medulla oblongata*. Death must have been virtually instantaneous.'

The coroner wrinkled his forehead. 'Is it your opinion that the blow you speak of was received at the same time as the other injuries?'

'Yes, your honour,' grinned Burney. 'It is clear that death

must have supervened shortly after the other injuries were received. There was very little spreading of the bruising.'

'There was no evidence of any condition – such as a weak heart – which might have been the primary cause of death?'

'No, your honour. Mr Potter seems to have been a very healthy young man, if a little undernourished.'

'Have you any indication of the nature of the object that caused his death?' asked the coroner.

'It was a heavy cylindrical object of some two inches diameter – say, an iron bar, or a weighted club.'

The coroner nodded to a juror who was holding up his hand. 'I would like to ask the witness, your honour, if it were possible that the deceased had been engaging in fisticuffs, and struck his head when he was knocked down.'

'I am not an expert in pugilism,' beamed Burney, 'but there was extensive bruising round the kidneys and genitalia, which could not have occurred in a bout under the Queensberry Rules as I understand them. As to the question of a contest in the old style, without gloves, I would say that it was in the highest degree improbable. I examined the skin of the deceased's hands with some care. There was a small laceration on the first knuckle, and associated bruising, but beyond that nothing. He clearly received far more punishment than he was able to deliver. In addition I observed local bruising on the wrists, suggesting that they had been grasped with considerable pressure for some time. It is possible that his arms were held during the attack.'

'Your honour,' blurted out a juror on the back row, 'is it possible that the blow the doctor described could have been an accident?'

'I think I had better rephrase the question,' said the coroner with a desiccated smile. 'Otherwise, in replying, the witness will be usurping your function. Dr Burney, if we ignore for the moment the possibility of a large iron bar falling from the sky upon this hapless young man's head, and assume that the injury to the back of the skull was inflicted by some human agency, does it have the characteristics of a deliberate attempt to cause serious injury or death?'

'The blow in question,' said Burney, beaming again, 'was of an entirely different order of magnitude from the others. Because of the force used, it was clearly intended to cause serious injury. As to whether it was intended to cause death, I cannot pass any opinion. What I can say, however, is that if I were intending to cause immediate death by one blow from a blunt instrument, I would choose that part of the body before any other.'

The coroner nodded his thanks, and Burney strode briskly from the court, leaving a loose Cheshire-cat smile hanging in the air behind him.

'Who is the detective officer assigned to the case?' asked the coroner.

'Sergeant Bragg, your honour.'

Bragg walked purposefully to the witness-box and took the oath.

'Have you examined the place where this young man's body was found, sergeant?'

'Yes, your honour. The railway arch is closed in by buildings at each end, with only a narrow pathway running through it along one side. The rest of the space is used by costers to leave their barrows, empty boxes and suchlike. As it is sheltered and dry, there is a thick accumulation of dust in the unused areas such as the corner where the body was found. I examined the surface of the cobblestones in that area, and found that the dust had recently been disturbed by many feet.'

'Were there any bloodstains?' asked the coroner.

'Not in the place where the body was found,' replied Bragg, 'but I discovered a small bloodstain, approximately three inches in extent, by some orange boxes nearby. It appeared that the deceased had lain there for some time while he was still alive.'

'Did you see any object which might have caused this injury?'

'No, your honour, I searched the whole court and the adjoining streets, but found nothing.'

'You see,' the coroner continued, wrinkling his nose, 'we have the problem that the body was cold when the constable found it. Now Dr Burney puts the time of death at between half past six and half past eight that evening. If we ignore the bloodstain, it's clearly possible that Potter died some- where else, and that the corpse was conveyed to the court after the constable passed through it at around nine o'clock.'

'In my view,' replied Bragg, choosing his words with care, 'Mr Potter was killed in French Ordinary Court at approxi- mately half past seven that evening. A constable thought he had seen the deceased in Minories soon after seven o'clock. Because of the fog he could not be certain of his identifica- tion, but the man concerned turned off in the direction of French Ordinary.'

'Is the constable going to give evidence?' asked the coro- ner, peering over the edge of his desk at his clerk.

'It was Constable Tait, your honour,' said Bragg.

The coroner sat up with a jerk. 'It's strange he didn't give evidence on this point earlier,' he commented in an acidulate tone. 'Is he still in court?'

He sat tapping his pen on his desk while a search was made of the building, but Tait had gone. 'Oh well, we shall have to do what we can with hearsay,' he complained. 'Was this man alone, or with others?'

'Alone, your honour.'

'Did the constable see anyone following after him?'

'Apparently not. We have questioned the proprietors of all the shops and public houses, but none of them remembers seeing him on that evening. We are also asking all travellers to and from Fenchurch Street Station on trains around seven o'clock at night to try to recall if they saw anything suspicious last Monday. So far we have had no success.'

'If the constable was right,' said the coroner, 'and he did see the deceased, then that would fit in with Dr Burney's opinion as to the time of death.'

'Yes, your honour. We have checked with his employers,

and he left their premises shortly after seven o'clock that evening.'

'So that if we take into account the bloodstain, it all points to an attack as he was going through French Ordinary Court?'

'That is my view, your honour.'

'Have you made enquiries about the deceased, sergeant?'

'Yes, your honour. He was a clerk with a shipping company in the City. He seems to have been a sober, hardworking man, and a good husband and father.'

'Have you found any reason for the assault?'

'It seems possible that the motive was robbery,' replied Bragg. 'I found his pocket-book on the ground near where the body had been lying.'

'Thank you, sergeant.'

As Bragg returned to his seat, the coroner began scratching away busily with his pen, and a subdued hum ran round the court. Then he cleared his throat portentously, and turned towards the jury. 'Members of the jury,' he said, 'the law lays on you the duty of deciding how the deceased, Arthur Potter, met his death. By that I do not mean the immediate cause of death – which in this case might be violent contact with an iron bar,' the coroner looked around the court with a smirk, 'but under what circumstances he died. You should consider three possibilities. Firstly that he died from natural causes, such as a disease or condition which might have proved fatal at any time, and which did in fact kill him on that evening. Secondly you should consider whether he died accidentally, from some mishap such as tripping over and striking his head against a wall. Thirdly that he was killed as a result of the intervention of some human agency. In the last case you would normally bring in a verdict of unlawful killing. If, however, you feel that the evidence requires it – by which I mean that in your view it would be totally unreasonable to put any other construction upon it – you are entitled to bring in a verdict of wilful murder. To do that, however, you have to satisfy yourselves that the perpetrator of the deed struck the blow with the intention of killing Mr Potter, or of inflicting grievous bodily harm on him.

'Now you have heard how the body was subsequently examined by Dr Burney, who is Professor of Pathology at St Bartholomew's Hospital, and most eminent in his profession. You will recall that he described Potter as a very healthy young man, and you may feel that this is sufficient to dismiss from your minds any idea that he died from natural causes. Now you will remember that Dr Burney put the time of death at between half past six and half past eight on Monday night. Also you will recollect that Constable Tait is said to have thought that he saw the deceased walking towards French Ordinary Court some short time after seven o'clock – although Constable Tait had forgotton the fact when he gave evidence this morning. It has been said that it was a foggy evening, but nevertheless you may feel entitled to infer that if the constable really did see Mr Potter, the deceased had not then received the injuries which led to his death, since they would surely have been apparent even to him.' He paused as an appreciative murmur ran round the court. 'On that premise, you may feel it not unreasonable to conclude that the deceased was attacked in the vicinity of French Ordinary Court, or in the court itself, where the body was found.

'You may wonder,' he went on with a malicious smile, 'how it was possible for a body to remain undiscovered for two hours, when Constable Tait was passing through the court every twenty minutes – some five or six times in all. In view, however, of Sergeant Bragg's description of the blood-stains at the scene, and the medical evidence of the time of death, you may decide the fact that Constable Tait did not discover the body until half past nine is something you can ignore, and leave to another authority to take appropriate action.

'As to the deceased's injuries, you have heard that there were numerous bruises and lacerations, which might have been received in a scuffle, such as occur all too frequently outside the public houses of this city. The piece of evidence

that conflicts with this interpretation is Dr Burney's asser-
tion that his hands were barely grazed. You may feel it
inconceivable that in a drunken brawl blows would not have
been traded equally. You will also remember that there were
bruises upon the wrists of the deceased, and you may feel
that the evidence points to his being set upon by a number of
people who were able to restrain him, whilst themselves
inflicting there minor injuries upon him.'

The coroner sipped delicately from a glass of water,
before continuing. 'We now come to the blow that killed
him, and you will recall that Sergeant Bragg found no
object at or near the scene that could have inflicted the
wound. You may feel that this alone removes any possibility
that the death was accidental. You will remember Dr Burney's opinion that the blow to the back of the head was
struck with far greater force than the other blows.' The
coroner referred to his notes. 'He said it was of an entirely
different order of magnitude, that it had been struck with
prodigious force, and because of that it had clearly been
intended to inflict serious injury. You will also recall that the
sergeant found the deceased's pocket-book at the scene, and
formed the view that robbery might have been the motive
for the attack. Now, in English law, robbery is a felony, and
it is well established that where death is caused in further-
ance of a felony, then that is murder. You may therefore feel
that the only possible verdict open to you on the evidence is
that Arthur Potter was murdered.'

The coroner peered over the edge of his desk at the
foreman of the jury. 'Do you wish to retire?' he asked
brusquely.

There was a hurried conclave in the box. 'No, your
honour.'

'Are you agreed upon your verdict?'

'We are, your honour.' The foreman rose to his feet. 'Our
verdict is that Arthur Potter was wilfully murdered by a
person or persons unknown.'

'May I say that I entirely agree with your verdict,'
remarked the coroner briskly. 'I also wish to add an observa-

tion as to the conduct of the police in this case. For centuries the investigation of unexpected death has been the responsibility of the coroner's court. The conduct of enquiries into the cause of death lies with the coroner, as does the apprehension of any person who may have unlawfully killed another. In this the police are merely acting as the coroner's officers. There is a procedure clearly laid down for the coroner to be informed of any sudden death through the Ward Beadle. Furthermore, I have repeatedly stressed, since the series of horrifying murders in the Whitechapel area and in this City, that the police surgeon should examine a body where it is lying, before it is moved.

'In the present case we are told that the Beadle was not at home, though no message was left for him. As a result I was not made aware of the death until the morning of the following day. Not only was no doctor called to the scene, but the corpse was unceremoniously loaded on to a costermonger's barrow and trundled to the mortuary, without anyone from the detective division being called to examine it. I regard this as a deplorable lapse of duty, and I shall make the strongest possible representations to the Commissioner concerning it.' The coroner peered round the court as if challenging anyone to protest. 'The verdict of the court is that Arthur Potter was wilfully murdered. I formally direct the City of London Police to pursue and apprehend the murderers.'

West India Dock Road was so thronged with foreigners that they scarcely heard a snatch of English. Predominant was the twanging chatter of the Chinese, and occasionally they heard the melancholy vowels of Jews newly fled from Russia. Crowe and Scrutton had their premises in a tall brick building with a stuccoed classical pediment. Bragg rang the bell on the counter, and after a moment a thin stooping figure appeared. He was coatless, and wore black cloth oversleeves up to his elbows.

'Yes?' he asked bleakly.

'Manager, please,' said Bragg sharply.

'Complaint?'

'Police.'

Without further reply the man shuffled off. They waited for some minutes, Bragg trying to conceal his impatience by studying the framed etchings of tea clippers on the walls. At last they heard quick footsteps, and a man appeared behind the counter. He was about forty, well groomed, with a narrow moustache and round shining face. He wore a black morning coat and a gold tie-pin. He wasted no time in casual remarks. 'You say you are police?'

'Yes.'

'Can I see your identification?'

Bragg passed over his card.

'City Police? Well, what do you want?'

'We are investigating the death of a Mr Arthur Potter. Did you know him?'

'No, sergeant. Should I have done?'

'He used to work for the Cross Shipping Company.'

'In their docks office?'

'No, in Leadenhall Street.'

'I'm sorry, I didn't know him,' said the man dismissively.

'He was a book-keeper, and amongst other things he kept your account with Cross Shipping.'

'How does that concern me?'

'We have reason to suppose that the entries in the books may not be complete.'

'What's in their books is nothing to do with us,' he said sharply.

'How would you describe the account?' asked Bragg in a conciliatory tone.

'What do you mean?'

'Would you say it was conducted in the way you would expect of a big shipping company?'

'Well, we sell them a lot of goods – all the year round. They take the full month's credit, then pay. What you'd expect.'

'I'm going to ask you to let me have a copy of the Cross account from your books.'

'That's not possible,' snapped the man. 'I haven't got enough staff as it is.'

'I'll be content with the twelve months from October 'eighty-eight to the following September.'

'But that's pages and pages. I can't spare that sort of time. We're coming up to our year end.'

'Look, mister whatever-your-bloody-name-is,' cried Bragg angrily, 'I want that account, and I'm going to get it. If a copy isn't at my office in a week, I'll ask the Metropolitan to put in an army of bloody detectives to get it for me!'

'Why was he so hostile?' asked Morton, wrapping his chilled fingers round a mug of tea.

'A good question.' Bragg was cutting careful slices from a plug of tobacco with a juice-stained knife. 'There may be nothing in it. Not everybody regards the police as playing on the same side as them. Even a business can take on the attitude of the area around it – and Limehouse is a pretty tough area.'

He struck a match, and puffed like a railway engine. 'On the other hand there may be something wrong. If so, it may be our business, or it may not.'

'I don't follow you,' broke in Morton.

'There's a terrible lot of goods stolen from the docks, and they've got to be fenced. Some of the little chandlers must sell more loot than legitimate.'

'And that would be down to the Met?'

'Or the Thames Police.' Bragg tamped down his pipe with a calloused finger. 'On the other hand he could have been up to something with our friend Potter. Once you get a Judas in a customer's office you can sell the same lot of goods ten times over – till you're caught.'

'But he seemed to be saying that the account was run properly,' objected Morton.

'Well, he would, wouldn't he? Anyway, we shall have to wait till we get the copy.'

'Will it necessarily show the true position?' asked Morton.

'Not if they set it up carefully from the start,' replied Bragg thoughtfully. 'One thing's for sure, though, they can't get their heads together now.'

The remark jolted Morton. He had been impressed by Bragg's determination to re-create Potter's background, as if trying to put on his skin; and Bragg's concern for the widow had been real enough. Yet at the same time he could dismiss it all with a gibe. It wasn't so different from the surgeon's manner, an amalgam of sensitivity and detachment. Morton wondered if exposure to brutality would make him the same, his humanity atrophied.

'Well, now's your chance to do some real detective work,' said Bragg with a sardonic smile. 'With that page missing from the Scrutton account we're working on the assumption that Potter was a bit of a rogue, right?'

'That's so.'

'Then where's the swag?'

'Swag?'

'You've been in the house. No sign of easy money there. Rented, not much furniture – and that was the best room in the house, you can bet.'

'There was the holiday in Southend.'

'Exactly,' grunted Bragg with approval. 'He didn't save for that out of his wages. He's got a hoard somewhere, and you're going to find it.'

'How will I do that?'

'Your average clerk would keep his savings in a baccy tin or under the mattress, but remember Potter had worked in the City for umpteen years; he'd be used to business ways. It's my belief he has it stacked away in a bank somewhere, and you're going round every bank in London till you find it.'

'Good God! Wherever shall I start?' asked Morton in dismay.

'It won't be far away. He has to be able to get at it in banking hours, so it won't be at Bethnal Green. Being a City clerk, I'd be surprised if he went outside the City – they're terrible snobs! On the other hand he wouldn't be likely to pick a big branch, or one near Leadenhall Street.'

'But that still leaves a vast number.'

'Only about two hundred! Good experience for you, lad! I'll do the first with you, then you're on your own. Come on, before they close.'

'What makes someone like you join the police then?'

They were sitting by a blazing tap-room fire, the cold slowly ebbing from their bodies. Morton looked up abruptly at Bragg's question.

'I don't really know,' he said reflectively. 'I tried the gay social round for a year after I came down from Trinity, and then I suppose I got the feeling that I ought to do something with my life.'

He moved his glass thoughtfully on the marble table-top, spreading the beer-drips in a widening circle. Then he said lightly, 'I decided there was nothing more significant than upholding the fabric of society.'

'But why the police?' asked Bragg.

'Why not? Anyone would be privileged to belong to such a fine service.'

Bragg searched the handsome face for any hint of mockery, but its gravity was unbroken. He swung round, and grabbed the arm of a passing waiter. 'Bring me a plate of jellied eels,' he commanded, 'and one for my friend – and two more pints.'

'I don't really feel . . .' began Morton.

'Nonsense, it's food for the gods. There you are, a symphony of pink and silver. Ought to hang it in the Royal Academy – delicious!'

'It's not something I've tried before . . .'

'Then you've been missing one of the greatest gastronomic experiences the world has on offer.'

Morton poked in the jelly dubiously with his spoon.

'If you want to be a real detective, as opposed to just playing at it, you'll have to come down off your perch and scratch in the muck with the rest of us.' Bragg's quizzical smile took the edge off his words. 'You'll have to get to know the people you're working amongst – and that means the lot at the bottom, not the top where you come from. Now if you want to know your real Londoner, if you want to share in his pleasures, be transported with him to the very height of ecstasy, then you should sample Mackeson's stout – which they can't provide in this benighted pub – and a plate of jellied eels. When I first came to London I'd be down in Hoxton at McDonald's Music Hall every Saturday night. A pint of Macky from the bar, and some eels from the stall outside – ambrosia! The do-gooders have it now,' he went on gloomily, 'all sanctity and soap, instead of grease-paint and gin . . . Oh dear! I should have reminded you there was a bone in the middle. Never mind, you'll be more careful from now on.'

4

'Lets's have some hush!' called Inspector Youdall in a crisp, military voice. 'Now we're mounting this search in aid of the City Policy, and I don't want anything to go wrong. The villain we're after is a man called Joseph Ramshorn ... I'm sure you could invent any number of witty remarks about that, Johnson, but leave it till after.'

The room at Stepney Metropolitan Police Station was crowded, the air hot and smelling of stale sweat. Bragg and Morton had been given chairs by the desk, and ranged round the walls were twenty or so uniformed and plain-clothes men.

'Ramshorn is wanted for murder,' continued Youdall, 'and we have information that he's kipping down in a common lodging-house in Cranford Street.' He glanced at the clock. 'It's one o'clock, and he should be in his bed by now. Yes, Wells, I'm sure you feel you should be in yours! You ought to be grateful to me for giving you the opportunity of a quiet walk on a nice crisp evening. Anyway, it'll give the lodger a chance!' There was a dutiful titter from the men.

'Now then, Sar'nt Mills has drawn me this street plan, so pay attention!' Youdall rose and turned to the notice-board behind his desk. 'Here's the Ratcliff Highway running along the river,' he said, pointing with a nicotine-stained finger at the bottom of the plan, 'and here's Cranford Street running down towards it. Now you'll see there are several little streets and courts around there, but the walls are all ten foot high, so a fleeing man won't be able to climb them. The doss-house is at the bottom of the street, here, where it joins Ratcliffe Orchard Road ... Who invents these bloody names, anyway? I bet the only fruit plucked there is a juicy bit o' raspberry leanin' up against the wall! Now then, you

49

see Bere Street at the back of the kip? That's a blind alley, so all we need to do is to stop up these two roads, Plantation Road and Heckford Street, and we have him. Sar'nt Mills, I want you to station two men at each of the entrances. And whatever happens they're not to move unless I say so. We don't want another cock-up if he doubles back on us. I want a further two men in Bere Street to watch the back, and two at the doorway. Right, sar'nt?'

'Yes sir.'

'You will grab anybody who makes a run for it, even if he says he's the Archbishop of Canterbury. Understand?'

There was an answering murmur from around the room, and a shuffling of feet.

'Detective-Sar'nt Pearce and two plain-clothes men will come inside with me, and, of course, Sar'nt Bragg and Constable Morton as well. Sar'nt Pearce knows Ramshorn of old, so we shouldn't get the wrong man this time.' Youdall paused to light a cigarette, and inhaled deeply. 'You'd better come with me, too, Sar'nt Mills,' he went on, the smoke spurting from his lips with each word, 'intimidate 'em with your big shiny boots!'

Mills nodded.

The Inspector drew heavily on his cigarette again, so that the glowing ring crept visibly nearer his moustache. 'Any questions?' he barked, and to Morton smoke seemed to exude from every visible orifice – even his ears. 'Right then, off you go. And split up before you get there. I don't want you sounding like the bloody army! Sar'nt Mills, report to me in Bere Street, when your men are in position.'

Mills nodded again, and his men trooped out after him.

'Well now, Sar'nt Bragg, are you ready?' Youdall took a third powerful drag on his cigarette, and threw the spent butt in the fire. 'I'd like to have a bit of a snoop around before we go in.'

The night was clear and frosty, with a full moon that overwhelmed the feeble flicker of the gas lamps. There was no wind, but the dull cold seeped into the shoulder-blades, and Morton shivered in his heavy ulster. They passed a pub in the Commercial Road, its lights still burning outside, and the desultory sound of singing from within. In the warren of streets running down to the river the moon threw dark shadows across their path. The pavements were broken, the roads pot-holed and rutted. Sometimes Morton's foot would crunch through the ice on a puddle into the mud below. They passed deserted warehouses, with cranes like gibbets outlined against the sky. In every corner were piles of rotting rubbish, broken pots, rusty iron. To Morton the impassive moon only emphasized the grimy hopelessness of the neighbourhood. A rat scurried across the road at their feet, and Morton heard a frightened cry. He peered into the entry where it had run, and saw a woman crouching in a doorway. She raised her head dully, and Morton guessed she was about seventeen – younger than his own sister. He saw that she has hugging to her breast a whimpering baby wrapped in rags and newspaper. She rocked it clumsily.

'Shut up, you bloody thing,' she hissed.

'How old is the baby?' asked Morton.

'Four months.'

'Shouldn't it be inside?'

'Don't be bloody funny, mister,' she snarled. 'I ain't got no money, 'ave I?'

Morton took some coins from his pocket. 'Here, get yourselves into a warm bed while this weather lasts.'

She took the coins without a word, a look of hard excitement on her face. Then, hoisting the baby to her shoulder, she set off quickly towards Stepney.

'What the hell did you do that for?' asked Youdall.

'She had a young baby,' replied Morton.

'Christ Almighty! If you gave as much as a penny to every blower with a baby sleeping rough, your wages wouldn't last five minutes round here! She'll be up at the Admiral Ben-bow now, swigging gin. As for the baby, it'll either be tipped in the river or left on a doorstep before long. A child's no good to a whore.'

'But how will she be anything else, if she's not helped?' protested Morton.

'Don't be stupid, son. She wouldn't want to be anything else. They like it, otherwise they'd do something different.'

Morton thought he detected a half-smile on Bragg's face, and swallowed his retort.

'Go quietly now,' murmured Youdall, 'that's Cranford Street opposite.'

Two constables were already in position, and touched their helmets to Youdall as he crept past. From the end of Bere Street they could see the dark outline of the lodging-house. It was a long two-storeyed building, with a row of tiny barred windows under the eaves. The lower storey was screened by a high brick wall topped with broken glass. At some stage in its life it must have been a factory or ware-house, then, having been abandoned, it had been taken over as a lodging-house with the minimum of renovation. A gap in the slates showed black in the moonlight, and broken window-panes were stuffed with rags.

Sergeant Mills approached and saluted. 'The men are all in position, sir.'

'Very good, sar'nt,' grunted Youdall. 'Let's get in there, then.'

They sidled around the edge of the building, and were joined from the shadows by Pearce and his men. Youdall quietly turned the doorknob and they pushed inside. There was a room off the hallway, lit by a smoky gas jet. A kettle was singing on the hob of a glowing fire, and in front of it a man in crumpled clothes and carpet slippers was sprawled in a chair. He was snoring loudly, his slack lips shuddering as he exhaled. Youdall shook him roughly by the shoulder, and he gasped and grunted himself awake.

'What's the marrer?' he mumbled.

'Police!' said Youdall. 'We're searching the premises, and we don't want any noise. See?'

The deputy raised a protesting voice. 'What, again? We was done three weeks ago!'

'Shut your bloody trap, or I'll shut it for you!' hissed Youdall. 'Now what's the layout of the place?'

'Men downstairs and women up,' mumbled the deputy. 'We also got a few rooms for couples upstairs.'

'We'll start with the men. Lead the way – and keep it quiet!'

They followed him into a long whitewashed room, with a row of rickety wooden beds on either side. Pearce tiptoed to each in turn, peering at the sleeping face in the light from his bull's-eye lantern. Sometimes the man would turn over with a snort and resume his snoring again; mostly they remained fathoms deep in sleep. Bragg was at Pearce's elbow now, his eagerness turning to disappointment at each shake of the head.

'What's through there?' asked Youdall, indicating a door at the end of the dormitory.

'The tuppeny rope,' whispered the deputy.

'In we go then.'

They entered a low-ceilinged room with an uneven flagged floor. To Morton is seemed not much better than an outhouse. A stout rope was stretched across it, about two feet from the floor; and against it men were lying, back to back, dozing and cursing when someone moved. In the light from the lanterns one could see that their clothes were torn and muddy, their boots broken. Some of then had a bundle of possessions wrapped in cloth at their feet, one had a battered Gladstone bag; all were dirty and unkempt. Pearce began walking down the room, scanning the blinking, resentful faces. Suddenly a man near the wall scrambled to his feet and made a dash for the door. A thick-set detective hurled himself across, and smashed him to the floor.

'Is that him?' cried Bagg.

The detective twisted the man's arm behind him, and forced him to his feet. Pearce shook his head.

'Why, it's Bill Shand!' cried Youdall. 'They used to call him Billy the Cat once – but that's a long time ago . . . Got a guilty conscience, Billy? Cracked a crib, have you?'

'No, Mister Youdall, sir,' he croaked. ' 'Onest to God I ain't done nuffink!'

'What d'you run for then?'

'I thought as 'ow you was the missionaries a-comin' to save me.'

'Take him to the van, constable.'

'What for?' whined Shand.

'We'll find something.'

'I know me rights,' he protested as the constable began to drag him to the door.

'Scum like you don't have rights,' growled Youdall. 'If he doesn't shut his noise, tap him one with your truncheon ... Now then, sar'nt, any luck?'

'He's not here, sir,' replied Pearce.

'Oh well, better do the upstairs ...'

They crept through the still-snoring dormitory, and up the stairs.

'What's this?' demanded Youdall, indicating a door on the landing.

'A little room, let to a regular – Mrs Kent,' replied the deputy.

'Right, let's have a peep ... Hello! She seems to have some company. Well, well!'

As they crowded into the room, a naked middle-aged man sat up with a jerk. 'What? ... What is it?' he cried.

Youdall turned on the deputy. 'So you're keeping a disorderly house, are you?' he snarled.

'Never!' cried the deputy. 'I knew nuffink abaht it!' He shook his fist at the recumbent woman in the bed. 'Get out of 'ere, you filthy bitch, and don't let me set eyes on you again!'

'Shut up!' Youdall turned to her companion. 'All right, up you get. Let's have a look at you.'

The man hesitated, then clambered out, shielding his privates with his hands.

'He doesn't look all that dangerous,' observed Youdall.

'No, indeed I'm not,' the man cried.

'Name?' said Youdall.

'Officer, I beg of you to ask no questions, and let me go.' pleaded the man.

'That's an odd thing to ask a policeman!'

'Officer, I assure you that I am a respectable citizen, of unblemished character.'

'I like that!' brayed Youdall. 'Standing stark naked by a harlot's bed, and he says he's unblemished!'

'I beg of you, officer . . .'

'Stop calling me officer!' roared Youdall. 'Inspector to you. What's he got in his pockets, Pearce?'

The sergent crossed to the bed head, and took down a frock coat from the peg. As he did so, a bowler hat rolled on to the floor. The man darted for it, and, holding it beneath his paunch, seemed to recover come composure. 'There is no need to go through my pockets,' he said. 'I will answer your questions.'

'Right then. Name?' asked Youdall.

'Matthew Benson.'

'Address?'

'Twenty Bignall Street, Stoke-on-Trent.'

'Profession?'

'Wholesaler of china.'

'What are you doing down here, then?'

'I come down every month to visit customers.'

'And that's what you're doing now?'

The man shrugged resignedly. 'I cannot say that this lady is my customer.'

'Rather the other way round, eh?'

'It says in this letter,' broke in Pearce, 'that's he's a Sunday-school teacher down for a convention at the Baptist Mission Hall.'

'A Sunday-school teacher!' cooed Youdall. 'A Baptist Sunday-school teacher?'

The man hung his head. 'I did not lie to you,' he said meekly.

'You did the next best bloody thing!' cried Youdall angrily. 'So what are you doing here, then? Going in for a bit of transgression, are we? Or is it missionary field-work among the lost masses?'

'I was tempted, and I fell,' observed Benson complacently. 'God will forgive.'

'Hark at him!' exploded Mrs Kent wrathfully from the bed. 'After all I done! The dirty little prick!'

'That, madam, is your misfortune,' observed Youdall genially. 'Constable, get this worthy gentleman dressed, and take him outside.'

They entered the dormitory to find that some of the women had been wakened by the commotion. They had propped themselves on their elbows, shielding their eyes from the light of the lanterns.

'Right,' commanded Youdall, 'a quick look inside and under!' He stepped forward and tore the blankets from the end bed.

' 'Ere, lay orf!' complained the aged occupant. 'Bloody peelers! Can't even let yer sleep now!' She climbed stiffly off the bed and tugged the clothes back again.

Seeing what was to happen, the women began to squeal and chatter among themselves.

'Come in 'ere, love,' called one to Youdall. 'I'll keep you nice and warm!'

Morton approached a bed where a pretty young woman lay, her bare shoulders plump and smooth. She lay relaxed and still, her eyes fixed on his, a challenging smile on her lips. Her arms lay over the coverlet, and to drag back the bedclothes he would have had to insert his hand between her barely-concealed breasts. He felt a sudden revulsion, as if it would be tantamount to rape.

'Go on,' he whispered. 'Show me.'

'Ooh, I will!' She flicked back the blankets to expose her naked over-fleshed body. 'That's all you can have for free!' she cackled.

Above the hubbub there came a squeal of hinges and a thump from the far end of the room. Pearce dashed across and flung open a door. Morton could see a woman sitting up in bed, the blankets clutched to her bosom. Then Pearce shone his lantern upwards and revealed a man crouched on a cross-beam below a skylight. Pearce shouted: 'It's him!' and leapt for the beam. Ramshorn judged his moment and lunged viciously down with his foot. The heavy boot caught

Pearce square on the face, and he dropped in a heap, blood running from his nose. Ramshorn heaved himself up to the skylight, and, with a jerk of the legs, pulled himself on to the roof.

'Outside, everybody!' yelled Youdall, and pounded past the excited women in the dormitory.

Bragg put a hand on Morton's arm. 'Hold a bit, lad,' he said. 'We might see a bit more of the game from up here.' He flung open the window and peered out.

'I'll catch me death,' complained the woman.

'That would be no loss,' grunted Bragg. 'Keep quiet, will you!'

They could hear slow scraping noises on the roof, interspersed with shrill whistle blasts from below.

'Making for the eaves,' remarked Bragg. 'Probably a drainpipe . . . Yes, there he goes . . . He's on the privy roof now, probably jump down into the yard . . . No, he's not! He's walking along the top of the wall. Look, lad!'

Morton wedged himself beside Bragg in the window. A maze of walls stood out clear in the moonlight, and a dark shape slowly edging away from the building.

'What's at the other end of that wall?' asked Bragg.

'It must be the middle of Butcher's Row,' replied Morton. 'And there's no one there. If he gets across that, we've lost him!'

'I don't suppose that bullshitting Youdall can see him . . . Could we get there in time?'

'I doubt it.'

'See!' cried Bragg. 'There's a gateway to that yard from Bere Street. If we could get in there, we might fetch him down!'

Bragg tore down the stairs, and was tackled by the two constables at the door. One hung on to his knees, while the other endeavoured to pinion his arms.

'Get off, you stupid buggers!' roared Bragg, threshing about. 'He's escaping! Get on the privy roof and follow him along the wall.'

Abashed, the policeman clumped round the back, and Bragg and Morton found themselves in Bere Street.

'Can you see him?' cried Bragg as he raced towards the high wooden doors.

Morton ran to the other side of the street. 'Yes, he's almost level with where you are.'

'Locked!' Bragg rattled the doors vigorously. 'The bloody bastarding things!' He threw himself against them in a fury, but they scarcely moved. He ran across to Morton. 'Where is the murdering bugger? Christ! He's only got twenty feet, and he's away. Stop, Ramshorn!' he shouted. 'Come down and give yourself up! You can't get away, you're surrounded!'

The bearded face swung in their direction, then looked back to where the constable was beginning to crawl along the wall after him. 'Go fuck yourselves!' snarled Ramshorn, and began to shuffle forwards again.

'For God's sake, do something, lad,' cried Bragg in despair. 'I'd give my stripes to get him!'

Morton looked around him, then, darting to one side, he picked up a round stone, and threw it hard from the shoulder. It hit Ramshorn behind the ear. He cried out, tottered, then fell from the wall into the yard.

'Well done, lad!' cried Bragg. 'That was a bit of luck! Constable, get off that wall and open these doors, we haven't got all night!'

Youdall put down his cup, and wiped his moustache on the back of his hand. 'If you're ready, Sar'nt Bragg, we'll see what we've got in the charge room.'

He rose and strode into the next room. 'Well, well!' he cried in surprise. 'We have the pleasure of Mr Benson's company too. Got a ride back, did you?'

'I was brought here in handcuffs,' cried Benson, his voice quivering with fury. 'I shall complain to the Home Secretary!'

'I wonder how that could have happened,' observed Youdall innocently. 'After all, consorting with prostitutes isn't a crime . . . Mind you, if might be suspicious conduct in a man who professes to be a Sunday-school teacher . . . You sure you're Matthew Benson?'

'Of course I'm sure!'

'Have you a telephone installation at your home?'

'Yes, why?'

'Perhaps we should ring Mrs Benson, and ask her to describe her husband – after all you could have stolen those clothes . . .'

'No, no, don't do that!' cried Benson. 'I can see you have your job to do. Perhaps the constable made a mistake.'

'I'm glad you're taking such a sporting view of it, sir,' murmured Yodall. 'I'm sure we regret any inconvenience. You can go now.'

'Go? . . . Now?'

'Yes, sir.'

'At three o'clock in the morning! Where will I get a cab?'

'Well, we could give you a bed in the cells, I suppose,' said Youdall, scratching his head. 'But you'd have to share . . .'

'Thank you, Inspector, but no.' Benson got quickly to his feet and made for the door.

'Goodnight, sir!' called Youdall as he disappeared.

'Well now, Billy Shand,' he observed to the figure slumped in the corner. 'You see what bad company you get in when you go to these cheap doss-houses. You should patronize the Salvation Army, and run the risk of being saved. Come with me, and we'll see if we can pick a nice job for you out of the incident book.'

Bragg walked over to Ramshorn and unlocked the handcuffs. The man groaned and clutched his left shoulder. Bragg placed a chair near the wall, in the light from the gas bracket. 'Come and sit here,' he ordered. 'Where we can see you.'

The man stumbled to his feet, crossed the room, and lowered himself gingerly into the chair. 'You broke my shoulder, you bastards,' he gasped.

'Now then, that's no way to talk,' said Bragg. 'Where

does it hurt? . . . It's only a broken collar-bone. You'll live! Is your name Joseph Ramshorn?'

There was no reply.

'All right! If you want to play it the hard way. We know it is, because Sergeant Pearce identified you. I should think he might like to ask you a few questions. Do you know what you did to him? A split lip, three teeth knocked out, and a broken nose. He might think just one broken collar-bone wasn't much compared to that!'

Ramshorn looked dazedly at Bragg, biting his lower lip.

'Well now, we must do things properly, mustn't we?' said Bragg. 'So listen to this carefully – and you too, constable, so there can be no doubt it was said. Joseph Ramshorn, I must warn you that your words will be taken down, and may be used in evidence against you. Do you understand? . . . Do you?'

The man nodded.

'Got your notebook, constable? Right!' He bent down and glared in Ramshorn's face. 'We know you were in the City of London on the evening of the first of November with some other men, and that around seven o'clock you met a man called Arthur Potter from Bethnal Green in French Ordinary Court, where he was murdered. Right?'

'I don't know nothin' about it,' muttered Ramshorn sullenly.

'Oh you don't, eh?' Bragg walked past the chair, brushing the injured shoulder. Ramshorn cried out with pain, and started to get to his feet. Bragg pushed him roughly back. 'Sit down!' he shouted. 'You shouldn't make sudden movements like that,' he continued menacingly. 'Or we might think you were trying to escape, and then we would have to restrain you, wouldn't we?'

'For pity's sake, take me to the 'orspital,' groaned Ramshorn.

'Pity?' said Bragg. 'What do you know about pity? What pity did you have for Potter, eh?' He towered above the man, his face contorted with anger. 'Don't ask me to have pity on you!' he roared. 'I've seen what you did to Potter . . .

and I've seen his wife!' He took a deep breath, and controlled his fury. 'I want to know who the other men were, and where I can find them . . . and you're going to tell me.'

'I don't know!' Ramshorn grimaced with pain.

'You don't know, eh?' Bragg strolled around the back of Ramshorn's chair, then pushed by, jostling his injured shoulder again. The man screamed, his face twisted in agony, then he fainted.

'Here, hold him up, lad!' Bragg poured a glass of water, and flung it in Ramshorn's face. He moaned a little, and opened his eyes.

'Doctor . . .' he whispered.

'When you've answered my questions,' said Bragg. 'Who was with you?'

The man licked his lips. 'I dunno, only for Bert Carter an' a bloke called Lofty,' he gasped. 'Bert asked me along for a bit o' fun . . . I didn't know they was going' to do for 'im.'

'Where does Bert Carter hang out?' demanded Bragg.

'I dunno. I only met 'im at the Anchor.'

'Which one?'

'West Ferry Road.'

'Seen him since?'

'No. I reckon 'e's mizzled . . . Give us a drink.'

Bragg nodded, and paced round the room while Morton held a glass of water to Ramshorn's lips.

'What were you after?' asked Bragg.

'I dunno. Bert an' Lofty knew. I 'eard 'em saying somefink about a paper.'

'Did you get it?'

'I dunno. I was on the outside, singin' and makin' out we was drunk.'

'Who killed him?'

' 'Onest to God, I dunno. Somebody give 'im a quietener wiv 'is neddy, an' we all scarpered.'

'Who was it quietened him?'

'I dunno. I fink it was Lofty. I 'eard somebody tellin' 'im to lay off.'

'Who paid you for this?'

'Bert give me a tenner after.'

'That's a lot of money,' remarked Bragg. 'A lot of money for a piece of paper . . . But about right, if you want someone murdered.'

Ramshorn did not respond.

'Get a growler, constable,' directed Bragg. 'We're going to take you to Mincing Lane Police Station, where you'll be charged with the murder of Arthur Potter. After that, we'll let the police surgeon have a look at you. Don't want to disappoint the hangman, do we?'

5

'I must have been in fifty banks in the last fortnight,' remarked Morton. The bitter east wind had at last subsided, and as they walked along in the sun it seemed almost spring-like.

'How are you getting on?' asked Bragg.

'I've kept to the City so far. I divided it up into squares, and I'm working towards the river.'

'You're getting nearer home then. Don't get discouraged, lad, there are plenty left.'

'I know,' said Morton ruefully. 'At every one I tell myself "this will be it", but it never is. And it all takes so long. You have to wait for the manager to be free, then when he's instructed his clerks you have to wait while they look up the register; then wait again because it wouldn't be appropriate for anyone but the manager to tell you that they haven't got an Arthur Potter on the books.'

'That's bankers' caution, lad. They deal with the rich, and money demands that level of consideration. I'll tell you something, if we find it at a big bank we shall have the devil's own job prising any information out of them.'

'Why should that be?'

'Bankers are the high priests of the god of wealth, lad, and the principal canon of their religion is secrecy. They don't want policemen poking their snotty noses into their books. Our function is outside, keeping down the rabble, breaking up the demonstrations, making sure the social order isn't upset.'

'But isn't that right?'

'I don't know why I'm surprised that you talk like a bloody aristocrat, when you are one,' exclaimed Bragg. 'I suppose I credit you with some intelligence. If women ever get the vote, there'll be some upsets then all right.'

'I can't see it coming yet.'

'And do you know why? There isn't a politician in either party knows how they'll vote. They'll only get it when they take to hitting policemen over the head with bottles, and when that happens, I'm off. I was reading a book last night about ancient Greece. It was describing a pagan ceremony where the handmaidens of the wine-god tore the old king to bits. He was running away up the hillside, and they caught up with him and just pulled him apart. To do with ensuring good crops, it was, but it made Jack the Ripper sound like a Sunday-school treat. Here we are, let's see what our intrepid friend Smallshaw has for us.'

They entered the lobby and rang the bell at the reception desk. After a few moments a heavy door to their right opened, and the young woman slipped out.

'Do you want to see Mr Smallshaw?' she asked brightly.

'Yes, please, miss,' said Bragg.

As she swished down the hall he marvelled at the sheer joy generated by knowing she was young and beautiful. Just to have Morton there, gaping his admiration, was enough to light her up like a beacon. He thought of Daisy Potter, plump and white and lost . . .

'Ah, sergeant.' Smallshaw beckoned to them from the bottom of the passage, and showed them into the little room under the stairs. 'I've checked my reconstruction of the account with the version you got from Scruttons. There are a few discrepancies, and I've listed them on this sheet.'

Bragg studied the paper in silence for some time, referring to the books occasionally, and gnawing his moustache in concentration. 'Not much here at first sight,' he said at length. 'The dates don't always match up, but you'd hardly expect them to. The quantities and costs seem to tie up, except for these items you've listed as possible returns.'

'And the crate of crockery,' put in Smallshaw excitedly.

'Ah yes, the crockery – hardly a killing matter though,'

remarked Bragg indulgently. 'How long will it take you to clear up the remaining queries?'

'That will depend on Scruttons and our docks office. They deal with returns, and they don't always give us proper notification.'

'I'll see how you're getting on in a week or so. Meanwhile, you chase 'em unmercifully.'

'Yes, I will,' said Smallshaw doubtfully.

'I'd just like a word with your guv'nor before I go.'

'Sir Charles?'

'That's right, he's in, I think.'

'Yes . . . yes . . .' stammered Smallshaw, 'I'll ask if he can see you.' He backed out of the room and scuttled down the hall.

'He must be some kind of ogre,' remarked Morton. 'Smallshaw seems completely cowed.'

'It wouldn't take much!' retorted Bragg. 'What's the betting he's too busy to see us?'

Before Morton could weigh the odds, however, a glowing face appeared round the door.

'Will you come this way, gentlemen?' She preceded them with a conscious ceremony that turned it into an occasion. 'Sergeant Bragg and Constable Morton,' she announced, and closed the door quietly behind them.

The room was large and high-ceilinged, with tall windows overlooking the street. A fire burned brightly in a marble fireplace with an ornate mahogany overmantel. Under one window was a table, with a model of a steamship in a case, and paintings of sailing ships hung on the walls. In the middle of the room was a large mahogany desk, topped with green tooled leather. In its centre was an opulent silver inkstand, and to the left a telephone instrument.

The man who rose from the desk was of middle height, and powerfully built. Bragg judged him to be in his mid-forties. His jaw-line was firm, and his hair black save for a hint of grey in the whiskers. His eyes were slightly protuberant, his hands carefully manicured. With a gesture he invited them to sit down.

'I'm so glad you came to see me,' he said in a deep vibrant voice which complemented his easy smile. 'If there is anything I can do to help you in this terrible affair, please don't hesitate to ask. It's a disgrace that such a thing can happen in this day and age – and right in the middle of the City too.'

'It is indeed, sir,' agreed Bragg.

'I've always been a firm believer in law and order,' he went on, fingering a heavy gold albert looped across his waistcoat. 'You may remember that when I was Lord Mayor, I pushed through a considerable increase in the complement of the police, and I intend to raise the matter again in Common Council. The City has to be kept safe for people to live and work in.'

Bragg cut across the platitudes harshly. 'Have you any reason to believe that Mr Potter was dishonest, sir?'

'Why no, sergeant. Why do you ask?'

'It's clear he was murdered, and we caught one of the killers last night. Now we're trying to establish the motive.'

'Let me congratulate you on the arrest,' said Cross, taking a cigar from a humidor, and piercing the end.

'Thank you, sir. He seems to be something of an enigma, does Mr Potter. We are told he was a very sober kind of man, a good husband and, according to Mr Smallshaw, a reliable employee. But at the same time we think he was a bit of a rogue on the side.'

Cross inspected the glowing end of his cigar, and blew out the match. 'What makes you think that, sergeant?' he asked.

'Just little things here and there. For instance, there seem to be some discrepancies in your account with Crowe and Scrutton.'

'Yes, Smallshaw showed me the reconstruction he did for you, but for the life of me I can't see there can be any significance in it. Potter was just a book-keeper, he didn't make any purchases, he didn't pay out any money.'

'Who does the purchasing?'

'That's all done from the docks office. I only have a small

office here to keep the main books and deal with financial matters.'

'Who pays for goods purchased?'

'That's done here. The invoice is passed by the docks office and sent on here. We enter it in the ledger and send out the cheque.'

'Can you tell me who signs the cheques, sir?' asked Bragg.

'Smallshaw and myself,' replied Cross. 'So you can see that Potter didn't have the opportunity to misappropriate anything.'

'Hmm,' grunted Bragg noncommittally. 'Well, if anything turns up, we'll let you know. Thank you for your time, sir.'

Cross rose to his feet. 'In this matter, sergeant, my time is yours.' He opened the door with a smile, and offered his hand.

'Good day, sir,' said Bragg.

'Good afternoon, sergeant.'

'A real politician, that one,' remarked Bragg. 'It would take a lot to knock him off his perch.'

They were drinking strong tea in a corner café with a view down Leadenhall Street.

'I'm not sure that I agree with you, sergeant,' ventured Morton.

'Eh?'

'I think that for some reason he was badly upset by your questions.'

'What makes you say that?' asked Bragg in surprise.

'It was his cigar.'

'His cigar?'

'Yes. He didn't take the band off.'

'Didn't take . . . You're roasting me again!'

'I'm not, I'm perfectly serious.'

'He looked calm enough to me,' said Bragg.

'Well, he would, wouldn't he? But it was out of character – he should have taken the band off.'

'Go on, convince me with your eloquence.'

'My impression of Sir Charles Cross is that he's what my grandmother would have called a "tradesman".'

'A tradesman!' cried Bragg.

'By that she meant a man who'd made a lot of money in commerce and then bought an estate in the country, so he could pretend he belonged to the old landed gentry. I get the same feeling about Cross. To me, he's a man who would want to be thought of as belonging to the very top of society.'

'I should think so,' remarked Bragg. 'After all, he's been Lord Mayor.'

'That doesn't necessarily follow,' smiled Morton. 'And I would expect him to cultivate their mannerisms and idiosyncrasies – in these days it would take him a long way.'

'So he should have taken the band off his cigar. Tell me why.'

'It's a kind of snobbery really. On the way up you stop smoking a pipe, and start smoking cigars. It's a badge of your success. The wealthier you get the more expensive your cigars, and you leave the band on, so that people can see that you smoke Corona y Coronas or whatever.'

'Go on,' said Bragg, interested.

'The trouble is that you don't have to be exceedingly rich to be able to afford the best cigars, so the really wealthy turn the gambit on its head. They smoke the best cigars, of course, but to show that they are of no consequence to them, they throw away the band – even before piercing the end.'

'Hmm,' grunted Bragg.

'I'm absolutely convinced that Cross only took that cigar to distract you, and give himself time to think.'

'So what do you propose we should do about it?'

'Well, if you look down the street, you'll see a cab has drawn up outside Cross's office. If he leaves in it, I want to follow him.'

'What would you gain from that?'

'It would be useful to know, for instance, if immediately after you questioned him, he went to see his solicitor.'

Bragg ruminated. 'All right,' he said, 'but for God's sake, don't let him see you!'

Morton had little difficulty in keeping up with the cab. The mid-afternoon traffic was congealed around the Bank, and he lingered on the steps of the Royal Exchange to watch its progress. The cabby must have been well tipped, because he forced his way belligerently into the centre of the mass, engaging in a furious altercation with the driver of a bus, whose horses had become unsettled by his tactics. Morton observed with amusement the efforts of a red-faced policeman, ponderous in his greatcoat, to free the tangled vehicles. At last he created a space for a carman who backed his heavy van a few yards, his horses' feet stabbing down at the greasy wooden blocks.

Now Morton had lost the cab behind a procession of buses. He dashed across to the corner of the Bank, and suddenly the cab was coming towards him, Sir Charles leaning forward in irritation, his jaw set hard. Morton pressed himself against the railings, dropping his head so that he could see only the hooves of the horse. To his relief the cab swung left, and he took up his leisurely pursuit again.

After half a mile Morton began to wonder where Cross was heading. They were leaving the financial and professional area, and the cab was firmly ensconced in the centre of the road. More worrying, the traffic was thinning, and Morton had to walk briskly to keep up. He ran to the cabstand at Moorgate Station. A solitary hansom was discharging its passenger, and he waited fuming while the elderly gentleman handed up the fare, meticulously counted his change and bestowed a carefully calculated tip.

'Up towards Finsbury Place,' Morton called to the driver. 'I want you to follow cab number seven five one seven. It went up there a couple of minutes ago – double fare if you find it!'

The cabby's face remained impassive, but even as Morton put his foot on the step he flicked his horse, and Morton was flung forward on to the cushioned seat. The cab swung into the centre of the road, and set off at a fast pace, seeming fated to collide with approaching traffic, but always swinging away at the last moment. Morton was worried that they would be marooned in the middle while Cross escaped them down a side street, but at least they were overhauling vehicle after vehicle.

Suddenly Morton spotted the cab turning left. He twisted round and opened the trap-door in the roof. 'Chiswell Street!' he yelled.

A moment later he was thrown in a heap as the cab swerved violently and rocketed after their quarry. Then they settled into an easy trot as his driver kept station behind the other cab. For a long time they went straight ahead, crossing a couple of main roads, and then took an erratic course through the side streets. Morton wondered if he'd been recognized, and Sir Charles was trying to break the scent. They were now so close that if Cross looked back he must inevitably see him. Then the other cab turned right into a narrow street and almost immediately stopped. Morton quickly paid off his cab, and was in time to see Cross rap with his cane on a door. He was admitted at once, as if he was expected.

It was a three-storeyed house in a Georgian terrace. The severe sweep of the slightly curved façade was relieved by brightly coloured curtains at the windows, as occupiers strove for individuality. On either side of the arched doorway was a railed area, with steps down to the basement. The street was clean, with young plane trees planted every few yards. Morton concealed himself in an entry and prepared for a long wait.

Now the chase was over his anxiety was transformed into exhilaration. He relived each moment, feeling ruefully at the bruises on his hip. At least he had kept up with Cross, and almost certainly hadn't been seen. He wondered what the cabbies thought, or if they compared notes after a chase like this. Pool all their knowledge and you could bring society down in ruins. And whoever Cross was seeing, it certainly wasn't his solicitor.

Then the door was opened and Cross emerged. Morton caught a glimpse of golden curls and a brief wave of a hand before it was closed again. Cross set off purposefully, without a glance in Morton's direction. Another quarter-hour passed, and then a girl came out. She was wearing a dove-grey coat with a small flower-trimmed hat perched on her golden hair. She walked quickly in the direction Cross had taken, and Morton followed. At the top of the street she turned right and went into a tea shop, taking a seat at a window table. She seemed to be well-known there, and was holding an animated conversation with the waitress and someone Morton could not see. He watched her for a few moments, and then, abandoning his vigil, walked briskly off in the direction taken by Cross.

The public library was new and imposing, but the best they could do was a Post Office Directory for 1887. It showed the occupier of 41 Charlton Place as Mr David Solomons – but the girl hadn't looked Jewish. He examined the current voters' list. There was no entry at that address, which meant that the present householder was not male. Morton sighed and took out his watch. The rating records might help, but it was now too late to get there before they closed. In exasperation he turned into the Metropolitan Police Station.

The duty sergeant looked at his card with some suspicion. 'City Police, eh?' he said slowly.

'That's right.'

'A bit off your beat, aren't you?'

'I followed a suspect into Charlton Place,' said Morton diffidently. 'I hoped you would be able to tell me who lives there.'

The sergeant scrutinized the identity card once more, then handed it back. 'Always happy to help out the City Police,' he said with heavy jocularity. 'Constable Evans!' he shouted and a fresh-faced young man appeared from a side door. 'This is Constable Morton, of the Swell Mob. He seems to need our assistance. Would you be good enough to oblige?'

'I want to find who's living at forty-one Charlton Place,' said Morton with a smile.

'That's my beat,' replied Evans in a soft Welsh accent. 'I just come off. I saw you hanging about in the alley.'

'You did?' asked Morton, startled.

'I'd have run you in for loitering,' grinned Evans, 'if it hadn't been the end of my shift.'

Morton coloured with embarrassment. 'I followed a man to the house, and I want to know whom he met there,' he said.

'I've only ever seen women there – one of them a real swank.'

'Could you find out who they are?'

'Yes indeed. They'll know at the shops. I'll ask tomorrow.'

'If you could telephone it to me I'd be grateful – it is urgent.'

Bragg tore a piece out of the *Tit-Bits*, and twisted it to form a spill. It was a still frosty night, and the kitchen fire was burning clear and hot. He jabbed the spill at the glowing coals and laid it across his pipe. Then, throwing the remnant into the fire, he leaned back into his armchair in contentment. In a few minutes he would pick up his library book, but first he'd finish his pipe – the first decent smoke he'd had all day. It was amazing how just taking your jacket and collar off relaxed you. Perhaps it was a symbol that the working day was over, and its problems would keep to the next.

He wriggled his toes luxuriously in his carpet slippers, and glanced across at Mrs Jenks eating a muffin for her supper in the other armchair. She ate delicately, taking small bites; but since she chewed rapidly and thoroughly it gave her the resemblance of a pet rabbit nibbling a carrot. Still, she was a cut above the rest of the neighbourhood. Her husband had been a dustman, with his own horse and cart. When he'd first come to lodge here, Tommy Jenks had lived in quite a style. Up at the boozer for oysters and stout every night. Tommy hadn't been any too pleased at his coming. Not because he was a copper, but because he felt diminished that his wife should take in a lodger. Bragg thought wryly that he was there instead of the child she'd have liked. Even after fifteen years she still scolded him for making holes in his socks or not changing his shirt. It was a godsend though, when Tommy's hand went septic and they cut it off. During the months while he'd lingered, Bragg had taken to forsaking his gloomy parlour and sitting with her in the kitchen, and after Tommy died he'd never gone back. Now they were sitting either side of the fire like an old married couple.

He wondered idly what it would have been like if his wife had lived. Would they have had children? Would he have been just as comfortable, with his pipe and his books? Or would he have been out in the wash-house soling the kids' shoes? What would she have turned out like? In their brief married life she'd seemed a bit feckless, rather overwhelmed with the bustle of London. Maybe she'd have settled down to it. It wasn't important anymore. Perhaps that's what made it easy to get on with Dora Jenks, each having been widowed young.

She had taken up her knitting, and the needles clashed together with fierce concentration. Navy-blue wool, thickish needles – something for him, obviously, and not socks because there weren't enough needles. He hoped it wasn't a cardigan. On past form she'd finish it sometime in July. Now a muffler would be handy, with these bitter east winds. Perhaps it wasn't too late to mention it . . . She was a comely women, really. A little plump, now she'd turned forty, and a bit of a shrew if you crossed her, but she'd still make a fine armful. Strange nobody had come after her when Tommy died. They probably thought he'd got his leg over. Perhaps he should have tried – she might have been a bit less sharp with him then . . . Maybe that was what she'd wanted all these years.

Mrs Jenks rose from her chair and crossed to the fire. She poked it noisily and lifted the shining copper kettle on to the coals. Bragg had only to put his hands round her waist and pull her on to his knee, and . . . He lifted a tentative arm . . . and there was a thunderous knocking on the area door. Mrs Jenks swivelled round in alarm.

'Shit,' muttered Bragg.

'Language!' she admonished.

'Well, it's bound to be for me, isn't it?' He pulled aside the draught-curtain and opened the door. A uniformed constable stood in the dim light from the street lamp.

'Joe Ramshorn's escaped, sergeant,' he cried. 'They want you to come down to Mincing Lane.'

'It all began when Jameson arrested this drunk,' explained the duty sergeant. 'There'd been a punch-up in the Wellington round the corner, and when Jameson brought him in a crowd of men followed. At first they were quiet enough – complaining the drunk had a watch and some money of theirs. They'd been playing cards they reckoned. You can see there isn't much room in here, and there was only me and Bill Preston on duty. So when they started getting excited I told Bill to take the drunk to the cell. That made them go mad. They were shouting and stamping at us, until I had to threaten to arrest the lot of them. At that they quietened down, and off they went. It was only when we went to look for Bill that we found him laid out on the floor, and Ramshorn and the drunk gone.'

'Is this the only cell here?' asked Bragg.

'Yes, it's no place to keep a dangerous man. They haven't done anything to it since the days of the Watch. If you'd arrested him any other time than Friday night, he'd have been remanded and safe in Pentonville. But you know how against sitting at weekends the magistrates are. He was due to come up tomorrow morning.'

'How did they escape?'

'Through the window, into the alley.'

'Where's Preston?' asked Bragg.

'I sent him home. He was looking bad.'

'I'll have a word with him. Where does he live?'

'Up at Bishopsgate. Number twenty-seven.'

Bragg walked dejectedly through the deserted streets to the other side of the City. After all the effort put into the capture of Ramshorn, it was criminal to let him escape. The stinginess of the Corporation was beyond belief. Not even bars on the corridor window! A child could have got out. He hoped to God they recaptured Ramshorn before the Metropolitan Police heard about it.

He was met by Mrs Preston with a mixture of anxiety and indignation, and shown into the bedroom where her husband, head swathed in bandages, was lying.

'How do you feel?' asked Bragg.

Preston forced a shamefaced smile. 'A bit rough.'

'Can you remember what happened?'

'It started with this mob following Jamey in. Seems they had it in for this drunk, see. They was pushing and shoving, and the sergeant tips me the wink to take him down to the cells, and charge him later. He stank of whiskey, and he could hardly stand up. I practically carried him down to the cell, and leaned him up against the wall while I got my keys out. That's all I remember.'

'Where did he hit you?'

'Back of the head.'

'Hmm. A neddy?'

'I didn't see. I expect so.'

'Did you see a tall man among them?'

'No. Nobody specially tall.'

'And the drunk?'

'He was a little bloke really.'

'Did you hear any names?'

'I don't think so.'

'Bert Carter, or Lofty?'

'No. I'm practically sure, but I wasn't there all the time. You'd better ask the sergeant.'

6

One of the barefoot urchins was at the counter when they burst in. Jock looked up quickly, and with a sweep of his hand stuffed what looked like a silver hunter into his pocket. 'You tell your father I'll give him his ticket when he's by,' he cried.

The child looked up belligerently, then, catching sight of Bragg and Morton, slid swiftly out of the door.

'Taken to christening watches in your old age?' asked Bragg.

'Just a pledge,' complained Jock. 'People should know better than send a wee child wi' a valuable piece like that.'

'Might get stolen, you never know,' rejoined Bragg sarcastically. 'Right, Jock, what about the French Ordinary murder? Heard anything more?'

'They say Bert Carter, Tom Geddes and Charlie Parker were in on it.'

'Any word on who sprung Joe Ramshorn?' demanded Bragg.

'Nairy a whisper, sergeant.'

'I'm going to nail those buggers, whoever gets hurt in the process, so pass the word.'

The bank teller was building columns of half-sovereigns, florins and coppers, ticking off the sheet before him as he went. Then he swept them all into a canvas bag and handed it to the customer in front.

Morton took his place at the counter. 'Could I see the manager, please?' he asked.

'Manager's sick,' said the youth, pulling at a pimple on his jaw.

'The assistant manager then?'

'He's out at lunch.'

Morton produced his card. 'Well, I'm sure you can help me,' he said casually. 'Do you have a customer by the name of Arthur Potter?'

'Don't know the name,' replied the youth doubtfully.

'Would you like to check the register, to make sure?'

For a moment Morton thought he would refuse, then he said: 'All right, just a minute.'

He closed his till and locked it, then went to a table at the back of the room and briefly consulted a large indexed book. 'What was the address?' he asked.

'Seventeen Barnsley Street, Bethnal Green.'

'Yes, we've got him,' he announced laconically.

'What accounts has he got?' asked Morton.

'Just the one – a deposit account.'

'Can I see the ledger?'

The youth looked up suspiciously, and Morton feared he had gone too far. 'What's he supposed to have done?'

'He hasn't done anything,' replied Morton with a reassuring smile. 'He's been murdered.'

'Murdered!' The youth's eyes opened wide. 'Oh well, I suppose it's all right then.' He opened a door at the end of the counter and beckoned Morton through. Then he took a heavy ledger from a shelf and flicked through the pages. 'Not much to it, is there?' he remarked, turning the book round to Morton.

The account had been opened on the second of June that year, with a deposit of fifty pounds, and the only other entry was a cash withdrawal of twenty pounds on the thirtieth of July.

'We'll make a detective of you yet,' cried Bragg in approval. 'Bottom of Minories, eh? Nice and out-of-the-way. When did you say it was opened?'

'Second of June.'

'How does that tie up with the missing page of the Scrutton account?'

'It's long after – it was February last year that was missing.'

'So it was. Well, that doesn't prove they aren't connected.'

Bragg got up and poked the fire vigorously till sparks showered down. 'That's better,' he remarked. 'I'm not inclined to dismiss Scruttons just because there isn't a discrepancy in their books that jumps out and hits us on the nose. As you will have appreciated,' he added, knocking out his pipe, 'West India Dock Road is as good as in Millwall. Where's that Scrutton account?'

'It's still with Smallshaw.'

'Blast it!' exclaimed Bragg. 'You waste so much time on a case like this, just checking and cross-checking. Give me a straightforward robbery every time.'

'It may turn out to be just that,' suggested Morton cautiously.

'It had better not! Inspector Cotton has been on at me for the last fortnight to forget it quietly. In his words, it's a monumental waste of time. Not that we can drop it with a Coroner's verdict of wilful murder.'

'But we have found the bank account now. You were right about that.'

'Yes, but what does a deposit of fifty quid prove? He could have won it at the races – he might even have saved it over a long enough period.'

'I suppose the withdrawal was used to pay for the holiday,' remarked Morton gloomily.

'No doubt. And yet it isn't quite right. A man doesn't save up over a long period for a holiday, while his wife does without furniture in the house. I suppose it could be a betting win, but that doesn't sound like Potter somehow.'

Morton felt totally despondent. Throughout the drudgery of the last few weeks he had convinced himself that if only he could find the account, it would solve all their problems. Instead, it was just . . . nothing.

'Don't get downhearted, lad,' observed Bragg cheerfully. 'Disappointment is very character-building. What is it

Browning says? "A man's reach should exceed his grasp"?
Always got a phrase for it, has Browning.'

'So what do we do now?' asked Morton.

'I think we might ask the Met what they know about our
friends Crowe and Scrutton . . . Anyway, let's get that
account back from Smallshaw.'

They hurried along in silence, hugging the walls to avoid
the driving rain. By the time they reached Leadenhall Street
their trousers were clinging dismally round their ankles.

'Oh, you poor things!' cried the woman when she saw
them. 'Let me take your coats . . . and I'll make you a hot
cup of tea.'

'I have a feeling the boss isn't in,' smiled Bragg as she
flitted down the hallway. 'Perhaps there's something to be
said for having you around, after all.'

Smallshaw came towards them, his face lit with timorous
excitement. 'I'm so glad you've come, sergeant. I've found
something very odd indeed.'

He escorted them to their little room. 'See, I couldn't tie
up this entry in the Day Book with Scruttons' account, so I
thought I would check back to the original invoice – only I
couldn't find it. In fact, I couldn't find any of that year's
invoices at all.'

'Still at the auditors?' prompted Bragg.

'No!' replied Smallshaw triumphantly. 'I thought of that,
and I telephoned them. They sent everything of ours back on
the twenty-fifth of October – they have a receipt for them.'

'Do you remember them coming back?'

'No, they were signed for by Potter – which would be
quite in order.'

'Any idea when the invoices went missing?' asked Bragg.

'No. There isn't anybody but Potter who'd need them.
And what's more . . . ' his excitement bubbled to the surface
again, 'the paid cheques are missing too! I decided I'd look
through all the records for the last two years, and the
invoices and paid cheques are missing for both of them.'

'When did you find this?'

'Last night. I was in the storeroom till ten o'clock.'

'So Potter removed the pages from the ledger, and took the invoices and paid cheques after they'd come back from the auditors?'

'That's what it looks like,' affirmed Smallshaw eagerly.

'Hmm,' grunted Bragg. 'And how are you getting on with the reconciliation?'

'Not very well, I'm afraid,' said Smallshaw, downcast. 'I've cleared this twenty pounds five and seven pence – it was a return we hadn't got a credit note for. And I think this seventeen pounds three and eightpence must be the total of those two items, though I can't be sure without the invoices. I shall have to go down to Scruttons and sort it out with them.'

'Then you won't need this,' remarked Bragg, retrieving the Scrutton account. 'By the way, who are your auditors?'

'W.J. Mason, twenty St Swithin's Lane.'

'Good . . . I may just pop in on them.'

Morton hung his chesterfield and bowler on the bentwood stand, and glanced round the shop. It was moderately crowded, which suited his purpose. After his long wait he would have preferred to be by the fire, but she had taken her usual table by the window. He walked slowly past, brushing her gloves to the floor.

'I'm sorry!' he said, restoring them with an apologetic smile. 'I'm not usually so clumsy. There's a bit of a squash in here today . . . Do you mind if I sit at your table?'

'Of course not,' the girl said.

The waitress appeared with her order.

'Tea and buttered toast with raspberry jam for me,' said Morton.

'Now why don't I have that sometimes?' enquired the girl. 'It sounds much more interesting than cakes.'

'My old schoolroom tea,' replied Morton. 'Time I grew out of it. You know, the more I look at you, the more I'm certain we've met before.'

'I don't think so . . . I'm sure I would remember.' She had a clear musical voice and hazel eyes. Her tip-tilted nose gave a pert look to her face, and there was a trace of rouge on her cheeks. Her mouth was perhaps too wide, but it gave warmth and spontaneity to her smile.

'The Lord Mayor's banquet last year, that's it. You were getting down from your carriage, and I almost bumped into your escort.'

'No,' she said with a smile.

'No? Then it must have been Lady de Grey's ball at the Savoy in May.'

'No!' Her voice was full of laughter.

'Then give me a hint.'

'Why should I?'

'It would be kind. I know! It was at Henley.'

She shook her head gaily.

'Cowes?'

'You're not doing very well.'

'Give me your name then.'

She pouted prettily, pretending to consider his request. 'All right, it's Bella Berkeley.'

'Bella Berkeley ... Bella ... of course! The actress! How stupid of me! You were in *Esmeralda* at the Gaiety. My first year down from Cambridge, I went every Saturday night. I was in love with you for a whole winter ... from the second row of the stalls!'

'I'm sure!' said Bella dubiously.

'It's true! I used to fight my way to the stage door, but Tierney would never let me in. Not being a masher, I didn't know that a half-guinea would have done the trick.'

'Why didn't you send me a note?' asked Bella, beginning to believe him.

'I hadn't the courage ... and then my mother fell ill, and I had to go to Kent every weekend.'

'Oh,' she breathed, sympathetically.

'And when I next went, you'd gone!'

'I left the Gaiety because George Edwardes said my legs were too short.' She swivelled round and extended a leg into the aisle, hitching up her dress to display her ankle. 'I can't see anything wrong with them,' she laughed, cocking her head on one side to watch Morton's reaction.

He inspected the ankle attentively. 'No indeed!' he said.

Their eyes met, and they both laughed.

'And what do you do?' she asked, delicately sipping her tea.

'Oh, nothing exciting at all. I've gone into the family stockbroking firm.'

'Is that good?'

'It's rather dull, but when I become a partner, I suppose I shall be making a fair amount of money.'

'And when will that be?'

'At the end of next year – if I keep on the right side of the guv'nor.'

Bella studied him speculatively. 'What's the name of your firm?' she asked.

'Er . . . Alexander Calthrop and Son.'

'And are you the son?'

'Oh no! The Calthrops have died out long ago. My name's James Morton.'

'We shall know all about each other if we keep this up,' she laughed.

'I'd very much like to,' he said earnestly.

'Like to what?'

'To keep it up.'

She regarded him with a quizzical smile.

'After all,' he added, 'you owe me at least one dinner from three years ago.'

'We'll see,' she said with a coquettish smile. 'Anyway, I will let you walk me home.'

As they strolled slowly down the street, her hand on his arm, Morton was elated. He had done his homework, and it was going well. Besides that, she looked worth cultivating for other excellent reasons. He was glad that he'd told her the truth about himself where he could. There was no doubt she was extremely attractive, and totally friendly. Unlike the society girls he'd met, who wanted a marriage contract on the table before they'd go beyond a decorous smile. Not that the comparison was exactly fair, but it seemed a pity that someone like Bella was so much more fun.

'What's the sigh for?' she asked, pouting her displeasure.

'It's just . . . that at the end of this short walk, I may never see you again.'

'I didn't say that,' she replied, mollified.

'You must be very successful to be living here,' remarked Morton.

'Don't be silly,' she said with a scornful laugh. 'You know how chorus-girls live. I'm no Marie Tempest. I haven't been on the stage for a year. And as long as my gentleman friend pays the rent, I shan't ever set foot on it again!'

Though he had anticipated the awkwardness of the moment, his carefully rehearsed response eluded him. 'It looks as if I'm out of luck again,' he said.

'You never know,' she replied with forced brightness. 'I may be back on the boards sooner than you think.'

They had reached her door, and she turned to face him. 'Thank you for walking me home.'

'Aren't you going to invite me in – to get warm?' he smiled.

'My gentleman friend might not like it,' she exclaimed pertly.

'Does he matter so much?'

'What time is it?'

He unbuttoned his coat and pulled out his gold hunter. 'Twenty-five to six.'

'He won't come now.' She frowned in indecision.

'Well, then?'

'All right, but you've got to behave yourself!'

She showed him into the parlour, and went upstairs. He dutifully warmed his back at the fire and studied the room. It was furnished with expensive pieces, and the carpet was deep and resilient. There was a recent photograph of Bella on the Pembroke table behind the sofa, and a leafy plant cascaded down the what-not in the corner. Otherwise the room looked like a furniture display; opulent, but without personality. He looked around for a picture of Cross, but there wasn't one. On a small table behind the door stood a telephone instrument. So that was how she'd known Cross was coming. He picked up her photograph. It had been taken slightly out of focus, and with her parted lips she looked soft and inviting.

'Looking at my picture?' she asked as she swept smiling into the room. She had re-done her hair and face.

'Can I have it?'

'Not that one,' she said. 'But I'll tell you what, I'll get them to do another print, and you can have it for Christmas if you're a good boy.'

'May I see you then?' he asked eagerly.

'Not over Christmas,' she pouted, 'I might be wanted then . . . But after Christmas my gentleman friend is going on a cruise in his yacht. I shall have all the time in the world then.'

'But that's an age!' expostulated Morton. 'Surely I can see you before then?'

'He usually rings up about four if he's coming,' she said. 'Can you get off in the day?'

'Yes, any time.'

'As long as I'm back by four. And if he rings earlier Alice will have to say I've gone shopping.'

'Who's Alice?'

'My old dresser. She lives here with me.'

'What about tomorrow?'

'Goodness, you are in a hurry!'

'I've been waiting for three years.'

'All right, you can take me out for lunch.'

'Marvellous! I'll call for you at twelve.'

'No.' She placed her hand on his lapel, and lifted her face to his. 'I'll meet you in the entrance to the library. Now go!'

7

Bragg found himself intensely irritated by Morton's story, without being able to justify his annoyance to himself. If Cross were involved – and it was a very big if – then Bella would be a useful source of information; if not, she was just a harmless acquaintance. The regulations prohibited policemen from holding chat with young women while on duty, of course, but that was directed at the man on the beat – and couldn't be enforced anyway. If Bragg objected to what Morton had done, he would only reply that no avenue should be left unexplored. It was Bragg's own approach, and he'd rammed it into the lad constantly. Whatever he said, he'd be in the wrong. If it got out, they'd say he was jealous of Morton – as if he cared about women! Yet perhaps it was true in a twisted kind of way. If only Morton hadn't described Bella with such relish! After all these years he ought to have come to terms with these feelings – and so he had in a way. He was content enough with his life as it was; and yet every now and again something like this would get under his guard, and cleave him apart.

'You know,' he said gruffly, 'I don't buy Smallshaw's theory about Potter.'

'I don't understand, sergeant,' said Morton, bewildered. He had expected some commendation – at very least a discussion of the use to be made of his acquaintance with Bella.

'What could he hope to gain from taking the invoices and paid cheques?' asked Bragg. 'The invoices have already been entered in the Day Book, and the bank has the details of the cheques, and, to cap it all, the auditors have seen them, and they'd have notes in their files.'

'Perhaps he did it to distract us from something else.'

'Maybe,' pondered Bragg. 'No, it doesn't really stand up.

You're starting from where we are now, not from where he was then. He didn't know we'd be poking around. From what Smallshaw said he could have left the invoices in the storeroom till kingdom come without anyone else even thinking about them.'

'Perhaps something happened to make him think that whatever he'd done was about to be discovered,' suggested Morton. 'He might have taken them to give himself a few weeks' time.'

'But why take the lot?' asked Bragg crossly. 'He need only have pinched the Scrutton invoices and paid cheques, and he'd have been just as safe – safer!'

'Perhaps he didn't have the time, they'd only been back from the auditors for a few days. Maybe he was going to decamp.'

'It could be, but not for a lousy crate of crockery – or fifty quid last June . . . There's got to be something else . . .' muttered Bragg.

Morton could see him drifting into another ill-humoured reverie. 'What should I do about Sir Charles Cross?' he asked.

'Still want to keep tabs on him, do you?' asked Bragg sourly.

'We do know that he intends to go on a cruise . . .'

'Well, believe it or not, lad, we can check that without hanging round his judy.'

Morton hid his chagrin under a wry smile. 'What do I do?' he asked.

'Look in Lloyd's List every day – or better still pop into Lloyd's. That way you'll know when he's sailed as soon as he does.'

'You'd better give me the address,' said Morton, carefully tearing a leaf out of a report book.

Bragg sprang to his feet with a shout. 'That's it! God Almighty, what a stupid bugger I am! Come on, lad!' He flung open the door, and raced down the stairs without even pausing for his hat.

'We've been on the wrong track, Mr Smallshaw!' announced Bragg jubilantly. 'He's had us chasing our own tails. See,' he went on, seizing the heavy ledger. 'We've been busy reconstructing this page, and we never thought to ask ourselves about the other half of the sheet!'

'What other half?' asked Smallshaw, cowed by Bragg's exuberance.

'This ledger's made up of sections, right?' said Bragg, pulling at the binding with his thick fingers. 'And each section is made up of several sheets folded in the middle. So if you tear out a page, there will be a corresponding loose page in that section.'

There was a sharp crack as the spine of the ledger split, and a look of outrage flitted across Smallshaw's face.

'This is where it should be,' cried Bragg levering up the section, 'but there's no loose page here. Where has it gone?' he asked rhetorically.

'How should I know?' retorted Smallshaw, with a flash of asperity.

'What we want has been on that bit of paper all along,' said Bragg. 'Now all I need is for you to tell me what was on it.'

'There might have been nothing on it,' objected Smallshaw peevishly.

'There was, I'm sure of it!' trumpeted Bragg. 'Now, where's the index?'

'In the front,' replied Smallshaw, retrieving his battered book. 'But the accounts aren't in strict order. Potter was slovenly like that. Rather than start another book, he'd squeeze in a new account anywhere. It will take time to find it.'

'That's all right, sir,' said Bragg exultantly. 'We've got plenty of time. We'll just sit here until you do.'

But Bragg could not sit. He prowled around the little room like a dancing bear, totally certain of the outcome, while Smallshaw shot him venomous glances as he turned the pages of his stricken ledger. At length he laid down his pencil. 'Charles Meyer,' he announced in a tart voice.

Bragg was at his side in a bound, noting the precise ticks down the index.

'I've been through the book twice, and it's not there.'

'Who's Charles Meyer?' demanded Bragg.

'A coaling agent in Marseilles.'

'Do you use him a lot?'

'I wouldn't say a lot. We only started with him a couple of years ago.'

'Would the account go on one of these pages?'

'I should think so.'

'Good! Then I want you to reconstruct it for me.'

'I can't possibly do it before Christmas,' complained Smallshaw. 'Sir Charles has me working late every night as it is.'

'Well, tell him it's urgent. Otherwise it'll have to be after Christmas – but straight after, mind!'

Bragg and Morton walked through the mist towards the river. The four turrets of the Tower floated above in the sunshine, while fog-horns trumpeted from the Pool. On the bank the fog was dense, and they had to feel their way to the ramp which led to the Thames Police pier.

'Sergeant Bragg, City Police. I hear you have a body for me.'

The oilskin-clad constable beckoned them on to the deck of a grey steam-launch, its brasswork stained brown by the fog. As they gathered in the stern they were joined by an elderly sergeant from the wheel-house. He gestured towards a tarpaulin by the opposite rail. 'We picked him up at five this morning. Bit of luck. He bumped against us while we were stationary or we'd have missed him. I'd seen the alert, so I thought you might like to have a look.'

'Thanks.'

The sergeant pulled back a corner of the tarpaulin, and revealed the face of the corpse beneath. Morton was reminded of a carved ivory Buddha on his mantelpiece at home. The same puffy polished whiteness, except that here the eyes stared in surprise and the mouth gaped.

'Yes, it's Ramshorn all right,' said Bragg. 'Have you told the Coroner?'

'Yes, the police surgeon will be down any minute.'

'How long had he been in, do you think?'

'A good few hours. He'd begun to get waterlogged already.'

'Where'd you think he was thrown in?'

The sergeant pulled at his whiskers thoughtfully. 'Well, we found him just below Tower Bridge, on the top of the tide. There's not a lot of land water at the moment, and the east wind works against the ebb. If he was put in last night, he'd be taken downstream first, and then when the tide began running he'd be brought back again.'

'Could he have been put in the day before?' asked Bragg.

'Not likely. There's a lot of shipping in the Pool, and as far up as Blackfriars. He'd have been spotted in the daylight, yesterday. No, I think it happened after dark last night. If we say eight or nine o'clock, so there's nobody about, he'd have had say three hours down river and five or six coming back.'

'Where then?'

'At a guess I'd say he was thrown in somewhere along Limehouse reach.'

'That would fit,' remarked Bragg.

'Sounds like the doctor. What's your interest in Ramshorn?'

'Oh, he was arrrested on a murder charge, and someone sprung him from Mincing Lane police station.'

'Well, well, Sergeant Bragg and young Constable Morton.' Dr. Burney stood on the pier grinning hugely. The constable helped him on to the launch and removed the tarpaulin.

'Good. How long has he been out of the water, sergeant?'

'Three and a half hours, sir.'

'Any obvious wounds?'

'Back of the head, sir.' The sergeant rolled the body over.

'Ah, yes. We've seen something like this before, haven't we, Bragg? Is that why you are here?'

'He was arrested on suspicion of complicity in the murder of Potter and escaped. Now he's got killed himself.'

The pathologist inspected the wound closely, then rolled the body on to its back. He peered into the mouth and pulled back the eyelids, grunting with amused satisfaction as he did so. Then he pressed firmly with his thumb over the cheek-bone and observed the dimple made in the water-logged flesh.

'Yes,' he smiled, 'you'll be wanting to know how long he's been in the water. I should say about eight hours – assuming he's been kept dry since you fished him out. That isn't necessarily an indication of when he died. I'll be able to tell you better after the post-mortem.' He turned to the sergeant. 'Will you get him up to the mortuary for me?'

'Do you think,' asked Bragg, 'that he was killed by the same man that killed Potter?'

'I should think it quite likely,' said Burney. 'The weapon is about the same size, and the point of impact is precisely the same. Yes, I would think it's our friend again. You'd better catch him, sergeant.'

'James! James!'

Morton turned, to see a brolly being shaken vigorously in his direction, and behind it a beaming face in a top-hat.

'George Denton! Good to see you!' he cried.

'Thought it must be you, though 'pon my soul it didn't look much like you. Changed your tailor?'

'My working clothes.'

'I preferred you in that fetching blue coat with the buttons down the front.'

'I've been transferred to the detective division.'

'Have you now? You're still taking it seriously then?'

'Of course I am.'

'No regrets?'

'None at all.'

'I don't mind saying everyone thought you'd gone mental, joining the police. Still, they'd have thought you'd gone mental whatever job you'd taken. I suppose I should be grateful. You and I are the only ones of our crowd who deign to plough the fields and scatter.'

'That reminds me,' said Morton, 'I'm afraid I rather took your name in vain the other day.'

'How's that?'

'Well, it was essential that I shouldn't be taken for a policeman, so I sort of swapped identities with you – said I was in your firm.'

'So long as I don't have to reciprocate. So you became George Denton?'

'No, no! I gave my own name. I just said I was an aspiring stockbroker. So if anyone enquires about me, I'd be glad if you'd back me up.'

'I smell a luscious bit of crumpet.'

Morton lifted an eyebrow. 'Yes, she was, actually,' he pronounced judicially.

'All right, but I shall want a commission. I may not have learnt much, but I do know a stockbroker does nothing without there's a commission at the end of it.'

'Name your price,' laughed Morton.

'An invitation.'

'Of course! Come to supper straight after Christmas, and we'll go to a show afterwards.'

'Splendid! Disperse the cloying effect of a family Christmas. But you don't get the idea at all, young James. The invitation I want is to Ashwell Priory.'

'But I'm hardly ever there. It would be much easier in town.'

'For a detective you're uncommonly thick, James. Who said I wanted you there? Though I'll put up with you if it enables me to spend an hour with your scintillating sister.'

'Don't be disgusting,' protested Morton. 'You've been with every harlot for five miles round the Haymarket.'

'So the devil is denouncing sin, is he?'

'Surely to God I don't have to debauch my own sister to get a bit of co-operation?'

'We'll have no more of this incest, my boy, it's weakening.'

'But why Emily?' expostulated Morton.

'Because she's virtuous – when you're out of the way; beautiful – or she was at eighteen; and she's got lots of lovely money. What better match could there be for a struggling stockbroker?'

'You're a buffoon, George. All right. I'll see what I can do, but only because I'm sure you haven't a hope – she'll go for a Duke, or an Earl at the very least.'

'I'll take my chance. By the way, how is she?'

'Very well. She and mother will be taking a trip to America after Easter, so you'll have to work fast.'

'Curses! I'd planned a long leisurely seduction. However, no doubt the Denton technique will be equal to the challenge.'

'You're disgusting, George.'

Denton burst into a peal of laughter. 'It's funny how chaps feel about their kid sister . . . I'm only jesting.'

'All right, George, there is something else you can do for me.'

'Am I not doing enough already?' cried Denton, beginning to laugh again. 'Bringing the old family firm into disrepute?'

'Shut up, and listen.'

'Oh, very well!'

'It's to do with family investments . . . Emily's trustees actually. There's a proposal for a scheme involving outsiders, and obviously we must know that they are good for their corner. We're happy about all of them except for a man named Sir Charles Cross. He's in shipping in London, and he sounds all right, but we'd like to be sure. Do you think you could find out about him for me?'

'You can rely on me. Don't want a penniless wife, do we?'

I'm so sorry I'm late again, James. I'd have given anything not to be, today of all days.'

He'd seen her hurrying from the corner where the cab had dropped her, and had met her at the street door. 'Let me take your coat.'

Bella slipped gracefully out of it, turning the movement into a joyful pirouette. 'This is lovely!' she cried, waltzing gaily round the room, and ending up by his side. 'I couldn't help being late,' she pouted. 'My old gentleman rang up unexpectedly, just when I was ready . . . I had to stay.'

Morton looked away in vexation.

'Now don't be a silly boy,' she coaxed, laying her hand on his arm. 'It's all right, he didn't want me. He hasn't touched me for weeks. He just talks . . . talks about nothing really. Then suddenly he ups and goes. I think he's got business worries. But let's forget about him. Show me your lovely room!'

She seized his hand and dragged him over to the table by the window. 'What's this box thing?'

'Open it and see.'

She raised the lid, and gasped with delight at the rows of little bottles within. 'It's beautiful! What's it for?'

Morton felt his ill-humour melting before the spontaneity of her pleasure. 'It's not for anything now,' he said. 'It's an old apothecary's chest. The little bottles would be filled with medicines, and the drawers would have herbs and things in – and I suppose the space at the bottom would be for his lancets and so on.'

'Has it always been in your family?'

'No, I bought it.'

'What for?' she asked in surprise.

'Because I liked the look of it.'

'How funny!' She closed the lid and surveyed the room, then swooped on the mantelpiece. 'Who are these?' she asked, taking down a photograph. 'I can see that's you . . . Is this your father?'

'Yes.'

'He looks nice. And is this your mother?' she asked, looking closely.

'Yes. She's very nice too.'

'And who's this?'

'My sister.'

'You sure?' she asked suspiciously.

'Of course I'm sure.'

Bella replaced the photograph, and, dancing over to the sofa, draped herself over it in a tragic pose. 'How's this for Lady Hamilton?' she asked.

'Fine if I can be Nelson,' he replied, putting his arms around her.

'No.' She pushed him away. 'It's after he's gone back to sea. Can't you see she's distraught?'

'I'd never go back to sea and leave you,' he murmured, trying to kiss her ear.

'Now behave yourself!' she admonished, swivelling upright and patting the sofa beside her. 'Come and sit down and talk to me. Do you live here alone?'

'No. Mr and Mrs Chambers look after me. They came with me from my parents' home in Kent.'

'The big house in the photograph?'

'Yes, I think they wish they were back there. They seem to go down every week on their day off.'

'However can they afford it?'

'Oh, I see to that,' said Morton. 'I feel a bit guilty about dragging them up here. Indeed I sent them off yesterday for Christmas.'

'And will you be on your own?'

'Till Christmas Eve. Then I go home for a day or two.'

'However will you manage?' she asked mockingly.

He tried to take her in his arms, but she squirmed to her feet. 'Show me the rest, before it gets dark.'

'Bella!'

'Come on!'

'Bella.' He imprisoned her hand and drew her gently towards him.

'What?'

'You won't need to go back home tonight, will you?'

She drew back to look at him, her eyes sparkling in amusement. 'I suppose it would be a waste,' she said softly.

8

After Boxing Day breakfast Morton took a gun, and with his favourite spaniel at his heels struck off across the fields, following the course of the river. It was a clear, cold day, with a light easterly wind, so that it was only in the most sheltered spot that the sun could soften the frost-stiffened grass. The cattle had been taken into the byres, and the wild animals possessed the fields. He saw the long ears of a hare erect behind a tussock of grass; a pair of pheasants were scratching industriously in the hedgerow, till they sensed his approach and whirred off clumsily. The spaniel whined in excitement, and Morton laughed and patted him on the head affectionately. 'Not today, old boy. The gun's only an excuse for a walk.'

He leapt across a stream, and climbed over the fence into a coppice. The rustle of his feet in the dry leaves disturbed a fox. He heard its sudden start and saw it running up the next field, its auburn coat glowing in the sun. 'Go on, boy!' he called.

With a single excited yelp the spaniel rushed into the undergrowth and disappeared from sight. It emerged in the field and set off in half-hearted pursuit of the fox, which by now was lost over the crest of the hill. Morton whistled to the dog, and sat on a lichened stump till it came lolloping back, panting and bedraggled.

'You're too old for that sort of thing, aren't you? I ought to know better.' He rumpled the dog's floppy ears and stroked its head, then picking up his gun he pushed his way through the brambles and into the field.

He crossed the river by the stepping-stones with the dog under his arm; a rook cawed its derision from the high elms. On the gentle slope in front of him a wide strip had been

ploughed parallel to the river, where the sandy soil met the
heavy blue clay of the valley. A flock of seagulls was forag-
ing in the furrows. Infected by some common fear or intent,
they suddenly rose in a white mewing cloud, wheeled slowly
on taut wings, then planed down to another part of the field.
He followed the footpath to the road, then turned left
towards Ashwell village. On an impulse he decided to forgo
lunch, and turned instead into the pub. It was gloomy after
the sunshine, and crowded with men from the village, some
in their Sunday best in honour of the Bank Holiday, others
in working clothes, fresh from tending the beasts.

'Why, it's young master James!' called an old man
ensconced in the ingle-nook.

'Hello, John,' said Morton. 'How good to see you. A
merry Christmas! You didn't come up to sing carols this
year. I missed you.'

'Ah,' replied the old man, winking at those leaning on the
bar, 'me throat's too dry these days for singin'.'

Morton laughed. 'All right, let's all have a drink to
celebrate. Have you anything to eat, landlord?'

'I've a nice piece of meat pie, master James, made this
morning.'

'Couldn't be better! And a pint of beer – I've walked miles
today.'

'Did you bag anything, sir?'

'No. I didn't even try. It was so good to be tramping round
the estate, I somehow didn't want to disturb anything.'

'Terrible lot o' foxes round here now.'

'I saw one in Ashley Copse.'

'With this hard weather they're coming right into the
village. Old Annie Styles had her chicken run broke into last
night but two, all her hens killed and the cock took.'

Annie was a widow, black-clad and shrunken, who eked
out a precarious existence with her garden and hens. Her
son was a cowman on the estate, and lived with his family in
a new airy cottage at the other end of the village. He'd often
tried to persuade her to move in with him, but she was
fiercely attached to her decaying little house.

'Tom says,' continued the landlord, 'that if he sees a fox he'll shoot it!'

'If he does, I hope he keeps it quiet,' said Morton, smiling. He took his food over to the ingle-nook and dropped thankfully on to one of the black oak settles.

'No,' said old John, as if nothing had intervened since his last remark, ' 'tis my daughter-in-law 'as stopped me coming. She's a Londoner. Hasn't no time for the old ways. Said I was too old to go gallivantin' about singing carols on a winter's night.'

'I heard your son had come back. Didn't he care for it in London?'

'Well, what d'you expect? All he'd ever done was farming. How could he expect to get on building houses an' suchlike?'

'What is he doing now?' asked Morton.

'Oh, he's labourin' at the tan yard.'

'That should be interesting. I used to love going down there when I was younger.'

'Interestin', maybe,' grinned the old man, showing a pair of yellow fangs, 'but 'ee don't smell too sweet!'

Refreshed, Morton re-crossed the river, skirted the boundary wall of The Priory, and, crossing the Pilgrim's Way, began to climb the steep scarp of the Downs. He followed a sheep track, winding like a white ribbon flung down on the short grass. At the crest he sprawled in the shelter of a clump of trees, and shaded his eyes from the declining sun. Below him Ashwell Priory lay in its hollow, the gilded weather-vane and tallest chimneys tipped with sunlight. It was, he supposed, an indiscriminate jumble of buildings, added through centuries to the medieval monastic hall. This was what he loved about it. To him it had vitality, exuberance, a sense of growth and continuity. It wasn't placed in its grounds like some Olympian doll's house, symmetrical, insipidly harmonious. Even the Palladian south front was awry, because his grandfather had extended one end to screen the new stables. The very clash of textures – flint walls, warm red brick, Kentish ragstone, cool smooth limestone – was exhilarating. It looked totally serene, with

the smoke rising softly from its many chimneys; confident of
its future, having weathered six centuries already ... The
sun dipped behind the trees, and, picking up his gun, Morton launched himself down the hill into the shadows.

They were finishing dinner in the small dining room. The
newly-installed electric lights drew out the richness of the
panelling. Throughout the meal Morton had taken little
part in the conversation, luxuriating in the lazy contentment
of being home again. His mother had recounted the latest
gossip, her soft New England voice reinforcing the occa-
sional barbed remark about village customs, to which his
father invariably rose like a trout to a mayfly. Now she was
discussing dresses for the New Year's Ball with his sister.
Emily was petulantly declaring that she was going to wear
her mother's *décolleté* black velvet gown, instead of the blue
silk dress that had been sent from London on Christmas
Eve. The argument would probably last for days, and end
with both of them going up to town for yet another dress for
Emily.

Morton glanced across at his father, sitting erect and
remote at the head of the table. His hair was receding fast
now, accentuating the austere integrity of his face. Morton
found himself wishing he could feel an easy affection for his
father, instead of the respectful deference he inspired and
apparently preferred. Sir Henry had spent so much of his
career in colonial wars that he seemed to be on parade even
with his family. Morton wondered what went on in the
privacy of his parents' bedroom, and then put the thought
from him guiltily.

He rose as his mother and Emily withdrew, admonishing
them not to linger over their port. Sir Henry took a cigar,
rolling it at his ear to confirm its condition. Morton watched
as the butler deftly removed the band and snipped the end.
Supposing he were wrong about Cross? Had he let his own
background impose a pattern that wasn't there? If he hadn't
mentioned the cigar, Bragg might never have considered
Cross a possible suspect. Yet on the other hand his guess

about the cigar had only been the spark, and there were questions still unanswered.

'You seem rather preoccupied this evening, James,' remarked his father.

'I'm sorry, sir. I'm afraid I've been wallowing in being back at The Priory. I'm intent on soaking enough into my pores to carry me through to Easter.'

'But you enjoy what you're doing?'

'Oh, yes. The detective division is what I really wanted, not directing the traffic and checking to see that doors are locked.'

'Are you still in the same unit?'

'No, no. We are centralized in the headquarters building in Old Jewry. I suppose it would be wasteful having detectives attached to each division in such a small area.'

'Yes, I can see that. What kind of people are you with?'

'I suppose it ought to be the cream of the force. I've been put under the wing of a great bear of a man called Sergeant Bragg. He's very experienced, and they say he's the best detective in London, but he's a bit prickly at times.'

'Learn all you can from him, my boy. I've always said that if things went wrong I'd rather have a good sergeant than a whole platoon of officers.' He took a sip of port, and tapped the ash from his cigar.

Recognizing the symptoms, Morton hastily changed the subject to avoid an evening of reminiscences. 'I had a most splendid walk today, along the valley and then up the Downs. This must be one of the most beautiful parts of England.'

'Of the world, my boy. I've been to every continent, including Australia, and I haven't seen anywhere to touch it.'

'Do you know what I'd like to do?' continued Morton. 'You remember Uncle Josh saying in his last letter that they are refrigerating milk straight from the cow in America?'

'Yes.'

'I'd like to try that here. He said it would keep three times as long as milk that wasn't treated. We're only an hour from

London, we could send it up on the train the same day. It's a tremendous opportunity.'

'But surely they have their own dairies?' objected his father.

'Three cows in a backyard, fed on hay. And the milk they give is watered down. The farmers of Kent could flood London with creamy grass-fed milk. We should put all the valley fields down to pasture, and install some refrigeration plant in the old barn.'

'It would be a great risk,' frowned Sir Henry. 'People don't change their habits easily, and it would be bound to be more expensive.'

'But it would be incomparably better.'

'Well, why don't you ask your trustees to buy a farm for you to experiment? If it's a success, I'm sure we would all follow.'

'The other land round here is too light for good grass, you know that. It would have to be The Priory land in the valley bottom.'

'In that case,' replied Sir Henry firmly, 'it would be something for Edwin to decide, and he always maintains he gets the best yield of corn from those fields.'

'And what use is that?' retorted Morton angrily, 'when it can be imported from America more cheaply? You are all living in the past.'

'That's enough!'

'Surely you can see arable farms aren't paying? If it wasn't for mother's money we'd be as hard-pressed as every-one else round here!'

'You're being impertinent,' cried his father. 'How many times do you need to be told that Edwin runs the estate, not you?'

'Edwin!' burst out Morton. 'Why don't we drop this farce about Edwin? He sits up in his room with a plan of the estate and that's about all. The bailiff goes through a pre-tence of consulting him, and then does what he thinks is best. You've relinquished control, and nobody is in charge. The only time Edwin lifts his eyes from his charts is on the odd summer day when there's no danger of his getting bronchitis, and then he's just propped in the corner of the dog-cart and driven round the estate roads. Do you call that running the estate?'

'Stop!' shouted Sir Henry, pounding the table with his fist. 'I will not have you speaking of your brother like this. Edwin is the heir to the title and the estate, and on my death they will pass to him. I will not have you interfering! Yes, he is incapacitated, but his wounds were received in the service of the nation, and the Queen. You should be grateful!'

'Grateful?' cried Morton, remembering Bragg and Daisy Potter. 'The only reason he was paralysed is that you insisted he go into the army, and the only benefit from that campaign is that we're likely to be involved in the Sudan indefinitely. Why should we be grateful about that?' He rose angrily to his feet. 'It's your fault he is as he is, and you pretend it hasn't happened so as to ease your conscience! If anywhere in your travels you came across an ostrich, you should be able to recognize yourself!' He stormed to the door and banged it furiously behind him.

Morton was sprawled morosely before the fire in the small drawing room, when he heard the door open and his mother dropped into a chair opposite him.

She kicked off her shoes, and held her feet out to the blaze. 'This is the part of Christmas that I like best,' she said.

'When it's all over?'

'Yes. No mere man could have any idea of the work that goes into it.'

'You should get Emily more involved. She would enjoy it,' remarked Morton.

'She's too young yet, all she's interested in is clothes and travel.'

'You baby her, mother. In a couple of years she could be married with a house of her own to run.'

'Goodness, you are cross this evening!' exclaimed Lady Morton. 'I hear you've been arguing with your father again.'

'I'm sorry,' replied Morton irritably, 'but I find the charade here more than I can put up with.'

'You mean Edwin?'

'The estate can't be paying. Granted it looks in good heart, but it's only because you are pouring money into it. And father pretends that Edwin is running it.'

'Edwin has little else to live for,' his mother said gently. 'I can't think of a better use for my money than giving him a purpose in life.'

'Even though the farming is hopelessly unprofitable?' asked Morton.

'Yes, even so . . .' Her voice took on a wheedling tone. 'Why don't you ride over to the Sommers' tomorrow. Louisa will be glad to see you.'

'No thank you, mother. I'm well aware that in your scheme of things my only function is to beget the next heir to The Priory. That at least is something you can't pretend Edwin can do. But I won't have you fixing me up with Louisa or anybody else. I'll marry when I'm ready, and it'll be someone I've chosen, not you!'

'James! This is churlish!' cried his mother angrily. 'If you can't come home without quarrelling with everyone in sight, it would be far better for you to stay in London.'

'Very well, mother,' replied Morton coldly, rising to his feet. 'Then let me say this before I go. However much you and my father delude yourselves, The Priory will come to me, not Edwin. With all the care in the world he won't live for long. If you want me and my family to keep it, instead of selling it to a social-climbing brewer, you had better take some heed of my views on how the estate should be run.'

9

'Good God! Look at this!' cried Bragg.

Morton crossed to his desk. 'What is it?' he asked.

'The Charles Meyer account. Smallshaw's worked all Christmas for us!'

'There aren't many entries,' observed Morton. 'Not like the Scrutton account.'

'No, but look at the size of them! They've been paid two hundred and fifty thousand pounds, over just short of two years!'

'I wouldn't have any idea whether that's reasonable or not,' said Morton.

'Nor I. No doubt coal's expensive stuff. We shall have to ask Sir Charles.'

'How do you think Potter could have defrauded the business through that account? Surely he'd not be able to put through fictitious purchases of coal?'

'Can't see it,' agreed Bragg. 'Cross and Smallshaw would have picked it up when they signed the cheque. They'd hardly let an item of that size go without checking it thoroughly.'

'Unless Cross was in on it?' suggested Morton.

'Don't be daft, lad, Cross owns the business, why should he swindle himself? This case has been the same all along,' he grumbled. 'Never anything you could quite get your teeth into. You think you've got a lead, and suddenly it goes and dies on you. Reach me that classified directory, will you – the United Telephone Company.'

He turned the pages quickly, running his finger down the entries. 'I suppose a firm like Corys might know, but I want to get someone a bit more specialist. Why is it they never put people where you'd expect to find them? Ah, here we

brains, did our Jimmy. D'you know, he's sixty-six next week? You wouldn't think it, would you?'

'How did you run the business?' asked Bragg.

'You'd buy coal in Swansea and ship it out to the coaling stations – by sailing ship, mind you! – and your customer's steamer would refill its bunkers at each one. The trick was to buy on longer credit than you allowed your customer, though it didn't always work. Once the customer's steamer reached Aden before its coal arrived. Light winds, the captain said, but he could have rowed it there in the time! Anyway we had to pay the demurrage. That cost us, didn't it, Jimmy? Still, over the years we've built up a bit o' stock in each bunkering station, so it can't happen again. Mind you, most of our trade's with the Navy nowadays. Steady, but they're mortal slow payers. Queer that, isn't it, the Government . . . ' Harris pursed his lips, and a frown creased the smooth skin of his forehead.

'I would have thought,' interjected Bragg, 'that Charles Meyer would be one of the big agents in Marseilles. He's handled a quarter of a million pounds worth of business for one customer alone, over less than two years.'

'It sounds a lot,' replied Harris reflectively. 'Who's the customer?'

'I'm afraid I can't tell you that, sir.'

'Well, there you are then.' Harris spread his hands and shrugged. 'It would depend how many customers like that he had, wouldn't it, Jimmy?'

The latter's attack had now subsided to a throaty wheeze, and he regarded his partner stonily, without attempting a reply.

'Thank you, sir, you've been very helpful,' said Bragg.

'Any time,' rejoined Harris, 'and knock a couple o' years off my next stretch. Remember!'

They regained the clear frosty air with relief.

'No wonder that poor bugger is coughing his guts out,' observed Bragg. 'I don't know how they can live in that stink.'

'There must be a tremendous risk of fire there.'

'Go up like Guy Fawkes night,' agreed Bragg.

'Just a minute.' Morton paused at a news-vendor's stall. 'I didn't have time to get a Lloyd's List this morning.' He began searching the pages. 'Damnation! It's been lying at St Katharine's Dock, and it's not shown today. Let's see what's in the sailings . . . There it is: *Athena*. It left yesterday.'

'Where is it bound for?'

'It just says "coastal".'

'That's funny,' remarked Bragg. 'Doesn't sound like a cruise. Let's see what we can find out from the office.'

'Sir Charles?' smiled the woman. 'Yes, he's in. Is he expecting you?'

'No,' replied Bragg, nonplussed.

'I'll see if he can spare you a few minutes, but he's very busy.'

'We're on the wrong foot here,' muttered Bragg.

She reappeared immediately. 'Will you come in, please?'

'Good morning, sir, the compliments of the season to you,' said Bragg expansively.

'Good morning.' Cross's eyes were red-rimmed, and the smile perfunctory. 'You wish to see me about something?' he asked.

'If you can spare us a minute, sir,' replied Bragg. 'I felt it would be helpful to get your views on the Charles Meyer account. You've seen it, I suppose.'

'Yes, Smallshaw showed it me before he sent it to you.'

'You're satisfied the account is genuine, sir?'

'Yes, of course, they're perfectly reputable bunkering agents in Marseilles. I've used them for a couple of years now.'

'Who did you use before them?'

'Marcel Chambière, but when the steam fleet grew he wasn't big enough to handle it.'

'Is there any possibility that Potter could have manipulated the account?'

'I can't see how,' said Cross dismissively. 'I would never have signed a cheque without seeing the invoice.'

'Suppose he were in collusion with Meyer,' asked Bragg, 'and they issued false invoices?'

'It's not possible. The invoice is checked with the captain's fuel report before it's passed for payment.'

'So he couldn't have benefited personally?'

'I suppose if he represented to them that he could do them some favour, such as paying them promptly, he might have got a few pounds, but it wouldn't amount to much.'

'Why do you reckon he tore the page out of the ledger, sir?' asked Bragg.

'I can't think why.'

'And the missing invoices and paid cheques?'

'It's my belief that Potter signed the receipt without checking the boxes.'

'Very likely, sir.'

'Anything else?' asked Cross.

'No, not at the moment, thank you, sir.'

'Then if you'll excuse me.' Cross rose to his feet and crossed quickly to the door.

'A happy New Year to you, sir.'

'And to you, sergeant.'

'Somebody waiting to see you, Joe' called the desk-sergeant on their return to Old Jewry.

'Oh? Who's that?'

'Dunno, a rough-looking cove. I'll send him up.'

Bragg had scarcely hung up his coat when the door creaked open, and a head peered tentatively round. 'Come in!' called Bragg peremptorily.

The man who shuffled in was clad in a threadbare coat fastened at the chest by its one remaining button. His boots were broken, and a stringy muffler revealed a collarless shirt beneath. 'Sergeant Bragg?' he whispered hoarsely.

'Yes, I'm Bragg. Who are you?'

'Mr McGregor didn't say you'd want to know who I was . . .'

'Who the hell is McGregor?'

'From Aldgate . . . Uncle Jock.'

'Oh, the fence in Spelman Street. Right, what's he got for me?'

The man peered down at his boots. 'It's about Bert Carter. I'm to tell you Marie Lloyd is on at Harwood's Varieties in Hoxton on Saturday.'

'I don't follow you.'

'Bert don't ever miss Marie Lloyd. Uncle Jock reckons he'll be there.'

'Good!' cried Bragg. 'Do you know him?'

'Yes.'

'Right, I want you up in the gallery. When you see him I want you to nod to Constable Morton here. He'll be downstairs at the back. Then meet him in the passage and point out Carter to him. Understand?'

'Yes,' said the man doubtfully.

'There's half-a-sovereign for you if we catch him.'

A brief smile touched the gaunt features, and the man was gone.

'Well, that's a turn up, and no mistake,' remarked Bragg. 'If we can nab him it'll make up for Ramshorn a bit. Do you know Harwood's Varieties?'

'I'm afraid not.'

'It's a small music hall with a gallery round three sides. There's only one entrance to the building, from Hoxton Street. You go into a passage and there are two doors on the left that give on to the back of the hall. On the other side of the passage is the bar. The stairs to the gallery are inside the hall, so it should be easy to seal it up. I'm too well-known in Hoxton to be inside myself, so I want you there at the back. It's a pity we haven't any other toffs in the division, you'll look a bit conspicuous on your own.'

'I'll take along one of my friends, if you like.'

'As long as he doesn't get in the way. I shall be outside among the market stalls with half a dozen men, and I'll have one or two more round the back, just in case Carter finds a window I don't know about. Now as soon as our unsavoury acquaintance points him out, you're to come . . . no, better still, send your friend to call me. I don't want to make any move till we're all in the back of the hall. So all you do is watch to see he doesn't escape till we come. All right?'

'Yes, I'm sure we can manage that.'

'Good. Now let's get back to today, and your favourite suspect,' said Bragg, laying a match over the bowl of his pipe and sucking noisily. 'The question is: can we believe what Cross tells us?'

'I suppose if he were implicated, it would have been a heaven-sent opportunity to throw suspicion on to Potter,' said Morton slowly. 'It must be in his favour that he didn't try.'

'True. But then if we'd checked the office procedures, we'd have known he was lying,' observed Bragg, striking another match. 'I think the wind's in the wrong quarter for my pipe today, too.'

'As you said this morning,' remarked Morton, 'Cross has no motive, so the fact that he has opportunity isn't significant. On the other hand Potter could well have a motive, but no apparent opportunity.'

'Apart from the few quid on the side.'

'Which could explain the deposit in the bank.'

Bragg knocked out his pipe, removed the stem and took a pipe-cleaner from his drawer. 'He didn't have any explanation for the missing account,' he observed, carefully inserting the cleaner in the bore of the stem. 'Wouldn't even hazard a guess.'

'Surely that could be in his favour?' countered Morton. 'Refusing to speculate on something outside his knowledge.'

'It could. On the other hand, it could mean that every possible explanation would sound equally unlikely.'

'He looked rather haggard, I thought,' said Morton.

'He won't be the only one in this great and prosperous city, this morning,' chuckled Bragg. 'I don't feel any too clever myself.'

'I don't think it's just that. Bella told me before Christmas that he'd been worrying about something for weeks. I think it dates back to the first time we went to see him.'

Bragg cocked a reproving eye at him.

'I don't like the way you're knocking about with that young woman,' he remarked heavily. 'If you go on, you'll find yourself involved with her, and you're just the sort of chap she'd like to get her hooks into.'

'You needn't worry about that,' laughed Morton. 'I'm hardly likely to lose my head over Cross's mistress, am I?'

'Apart from that, if Cross is ever charged, it will look bad that we got our evidence through playing up to his doxy. It's the kind of thing the courts don't like – and ten to one she'd never give evidence. That sort can be bought off with half-a-guinea.'

'She is our only source of information about Cross's movements,' replied Morton sharply.

'All right, but don't say I didn't warn you. Now if we can drag ourselves back to Cross, I didn't think he was all that sound on Meyer either. He said he changed from Marcel Whatever-his-name-was, because he wasn't big enough to handle the increased business. But according to our witty friend this morning, the size of the agent doesn't matter.'

He began to fill the bowl of his pipe with rubbed tobacco from his palm. 'And if Meyer is as big as Cross implies, then Harris ought to have heard of him.' He rose wearily to his feet. 'I think we'll send a telegram to the Marseilles police, and see what they can tell us about Mister Charles Meyer.'

10

'What can I do for you, gents?' Mr Green, the manager of Cross Shipping's docks office, was dark and stocky. His thighs seemed about to burst out of his trousers, and his rolled shirt-sleeves displayed muscular arms covered with tattoos.

'We are police officers making enquiries into the death of Arthur Potter,' said Bragg.

'Bad job that,' observed Green.

'Did you know him?'

'Yes, I knew him. Nice young chap. Bleedin' shame.'

'Did you see him in the course of his work?'

'Yes, course. He'd come down here often, when he had something he couldn't sort out.'

'I understand from Mr Smallshaw,' remarked Bragg, 'that the books in Leadenhall Street were a kind of check on your work, and that the two offices were kept apart deliberately.'

'Well, he would say that, wouldn't he? He's shit-scared of old Cross is Smally, but he knew all right.'

'Are you saying that the security arrangements were sometimes ignored?'

' 'S right. They've got to be, haven't they? It was the same in the Navy. I was bosun of the old *Arethusa*, and then in charge of stores at Chatham, and the rules had to be bent all the time. I expect it's the same in your lot. They're laid down by bleeders who haven't a notion how the thing really works, and as long as you don't let on, they're happy.'

'What would he come to see you about?' asked Bragg.

'Returns mostly, where he hadn't been sent a credit note. Sometimes he'd be on to us when we'd mislaid an invoice, and the supplier was badgering him for payment. Didn't often happen, mind you. I run a tight ship here.'

'According to Sir Charles Cross, he and Smallshaw see every invoice, and sign every cheque. Surely they pick up late payments? They'd be losing discount.'

'Well, if his nobship's happy, that's all right then.'

'What do you mean by that?'

'Well, old Cross don't know half what goes on down here. If he checked everything we buy, I'd never get a flamin' ship to sea at all.'

'What about when he signs the cheques?'

'If I send him an invoice, he'll pay it. He hasn't got any option, has he? You got to trust somebody.'

'And he trusts you?' asked Bragg, smiling.

'Yes, course. I wouldn't do the tight-arsed bugger out of a penny piece.'

'You've never been tempted to put through a concocted invoice for yourself?'

'Not likely. He'd break my bloody neck if he found out.'

'We were looking the other day at the account of Charles Meyer, the bunkering agent. You seem to pay him a very great deal of money.'

'Well, we would, wouldn't we?'

'Are you certain that account is genuine?'

'Down to the penny. That's one old Cross does keep his eye on. I reckon he counts the bleedin' lumps of coal!'

Morton and Denton strolled in a leisurely way up Hoxton Street. Denton carried a silver-topped cane, and wore a flower in his button-hole. In his pocket was a police whistle, which he was to blow if trouble arose, and he had solemnly promised Morton to keep well away at the moment of the arrest.

They picked their way among the stalls bordering the street, jostled by last-minute shoppers and drunks swaying out of the pubs. Despite the chill of the night, many women wore nothing more than a shawl thrown over a thin cotton dress. Some had no shoes, and trod unheeding in the mud and refuse around the stalls. Unwashed children lurked on the edge of the light, ready to dart in for an orange or a bun. A group of women was poring over lengths of material under a dim oil-lamp, feeling the stuff and anxiously debating whether the colour was right. At the next a man was selling second-hand clothes which had already endured several lives. He was surrounded by a crowd of women, feverishly picking over the rags, and haggling over a ha'penny. Morton saw an arm reach through the press, seize a shabby flower-trimmed hat, and vanish. The stallholder saw it too, crying: 'Stop her! The thieving bitch!' The other women ignored the incident and went on sorting through the clothes.

Further on a pot-seller had contrived an elaborate display of his wares, and was extolling their virtues in a rapid banter. 'Go on, treat yourself!' he cried, rapping a chamberpot with his knuckle. ' 'Ear that? Rings like Big Ben! No cracks near that – not till yer get it 'ome, anyway! 'Ere's one wiv roses rahnd the door, made fer the Duchess of Chester, only she giv it up! Fer three bob you can 'ave one wiv a mirror in the bottom, so's you can see wot yer doin'!'

Morton paused by a shellfish stall. 'Fancy some jellied eels?' he asked casually.

'Not now,' replied Denton. 'Sometimes I walk up to Whitechapel for them with the lads – I quite enjoy them.'

'You disappoint me!' said Morton, smiling at his own discomfiture. 'I think they are the most disgusting dish I have ever tasted!'

Denton cocked his head reprovingly. 'You're really too effete for this sort of thing, James. Now I have a real vulgarian streak in me; whelks and jellied eels come naturally.'

Bragg was standing on the fringe of a crowd round a butcher's stall. On seeing Morton he removed his bowler, and settled it once more on his head – the sign that all his men were in position.

Denton and Morton crossed the road towards the garish lights of Harwood's Varieties. 'Let's have a couple of bob's worth of the stalls,' said Denton loudly. 'I want to be able to see every lascivious bit of her!'

'Don't make too much of a spectacle of yourself,' whispered Morton anxiously.

'Nonsense! We're mashers, aren't we? Two stalls please, my dear.'

It was hot and stuffy in the crowded hall, with a huge coal fire on each side. Morton glanced up at the balcony, and saw Jock's messenger intently following the movements of Professor Alfredo Fantelli, the Dexterous Prestidigitator, who was relieving a portly and somewhat anxious shopkeeper of his watch. He placed it in a black velvet bag which he laid on a table. Then he took a large hammer, and struck the bag smartly. There was a crunch of glass.

'You lorst it nah, Bill!' called a voice from the audience.

'There wasn't no works in it, though,' shouted another.

The Professor ushered the hapless owner into a corner of the stage, and then began to juggle with hoops. He got five into the air, and, when he finally caught them, they miraculously threaded themselves into a chain. Morton at last caught the eye of the informer, and received a quick shake of the head. He looked warily around him and decided that half the men present looked like potential murderers.

By now the audience appeared to have forgotten the shopkeeper, who had given up even the pretence of smiling. As a final trick the Professor produced a rabbit out of a hat, and to the strains of the orchestra began to take his bow. The agitated shopkeeper dashed over and seized him by the arm. The music stopped, and the applause died down.

'Shall I give it back to him?' called the Professor.

'No!' yelled the audience.

'Make 'im wait till next week!'

'Let 'im 'ave it!'

The Professor silenced them with a gesture, waved his wand over the bag, then, taking it by the bottom corners, gently shook it. A jumble of broken glass, cogwheels and crumpled metal fell to the floor.

'O-o-o-oh!' cried the audience.

'Take it back to the shop, Bill! Tell 'em it don't work!'

Uncertainly the orchestra began again, and the Professor started to hustle the dumbfounded shopkeeper off the stage, shaking him by the hand with the words: 'Thank you for your assistance.'

'But what about my watch?' cried the shopkeeper angrily.

'Your watch? Ah, yes. Well, I wonder if this will do instead?" The Professor leaned over, and from behind the man's ear produced . . . his watch! The audience roared its approval, the shopkeeper ran shame-faced but relieved down the steps, the Professor made his exit, and the audience settled down happily. There was a rustle of programmes as the number changed at the side of the stage.

'Who's next?' asked Denton.

'Marie Lloyd.'

The informer was now leaning over the balcony rail, openly scanning the audience below. He looked across at Morton and, screwing up his face in disgust, shook his head.

'He's not come, it seems,' whispered Denton.

Then the limelights swung over, the curtains opened on a country scene, and the orchestra played a gay introduction. A hum of excited anticipation rose from the audience . . . but no Marie! The orchestra went into a tum-tiddle-tum-te, a murmur ran round the hall . . . and then there she was in an exquisite evening gown, sweeping breathlessly down to the footlights.

'Sorry I'm late. I got blocked in the Strand!'

The hall exploded into laughter, whistles and cheers. Marie waved and kissed her hand to the audience, then signalled to the conductor to start. From the wings, she took an umbrella and a battered little hat, which she perched cheekily over one eye. As the introduction ended, she made to open the umbrella, but it was stuck.

'Keep it going, George,' she called as she wrestled with it. 'I'll have it up tonight, if it kills me!' She winked, and a wave of laughter engulfed her. As it subsided she wiped her nose on her sleeve, ad began to sing. Swaying jerkily in time with the music, she was transformed into a rough, cockney child.

'We went gathering carslips,
Moo-cow came to me
Wagged 'is apparatus . . .'

She lifted an eyebrow, and the audience was convulsed.

'And I said unto he –
Rumptiddly – umptiddley – umptiddely – ay
Our little lot so gay
We don't care what we do or what we say.'

The audience joined in with a will, 'Rumptiddly – umptiddley – umptiddely – ay,' as the country adventures of this
cockney urchin were unfolded.

After a monologue, and a couple of favourite songs,
Marie retreated to rapturous applause.

'Let's get out of here to the bar,' said Morton. He paused
in the passage and beckoned the informer to join them.

'He didn't come?'

'No.'

'You're quite sure?'

'Course I'm sure.' The hoarse voice rose in indignation. 'I
could see everyone in the place, upstairs as well.'

'Is there any possibility you might not have recognized
him?' insisted Morton.

'Not a chance. He's got two front teeth missin' and an
'orrible squint.'

'Very well. Buy our friend a drink, George, while I pass on
the good news.' Morton found Bragg in a shop doorway a
few paces down the street.

He received Morton's report in silence. 'With our luck, I
suppose it was too much to expect,' he remarked gloomily. 'I
suppose they'll fish him out of the river tomorrow. Might as
well make the most of what's left of Saturday night. See you
on Monday morning.'

Morton strolled back to The Varieties. The interval was
just ending, and the bar was emptying rapidly.

'What now?' asked Denton.

'The sergeant is letting us all off duty. There's nothing much we can do, is there?'

'Good, there's a jolly-looking young lass over there I wouldn't mind hobbing a nob with.'

Morton turned to the bar. 'A whisky please – that's if you can change a fiver.'

'That's all right,' she smiled. 'We've had a busy night. Marie always brings in a crowd.'

'It's a bit surprising to find her appearing outside the West End.'

'She was born here, and she doesn't care who knows it. She's not after marrying a Lord.'

Morton leaned back against the mahogany counter and surveyed the scene. At the other end a solitary man was propped against the bar, gloomily intent on drinking himself sober. Morton watched as he unsteadily lifted his glass and emptied it, spilling some beer down his chin in the process. He wiped it on his sleeve, and began fumbling furtively in his pockets. He finally withdrew a small silver coin clutched between grimy thumb and forefinger, and rapped it on the bar. The barmaid unconcernedly pulled a pint and took his thruppence. The man stood looking bemusedly at the beer, as if wondering where it had come from, then took an exploratory gulp, leaving a spume of froth on his moustache.

Morton let his glance wander to the other end of the room. Denton was chattering away happily to the girl, who seemed amused but slightly dubious, as if unaccustomed to such frivolous preliminaries. Just inside the doorway a young woman was standing, clutching her purse to her, looking around hesitantly. Her glance met Morton's, but she didn't seem to notice him. She was quietly but elegantly dressed in the latest fashion, her hair carefully curled into a fringe.

'See you sometime!' called Denton as he went out with his girl.

The young woman was still looking about her, biting her underlip in concern. She was small-boned, with delicate creamy skin, and she looked very vulnerable.

Morton crossed to her. 'Can I be of service to you, madam?' he asked.

'You are very kind,' she replied with a pinched smile, 'but I don't think so. I only came to see if I could find anyone I knew. I've been cooped up for days, and I got so lonely I just had to get out for a bit.'

She had a low husky voice and regular teeth. There was no trace of lip-salve on her mouth, or rouge on her cheeks. She seemed totally out of place there, alone among the drunks of Hoxton.

'Why don't you have a drink with me?' asked Morton.

'Oh, I couldn't do that!' she cried.

'Why not? You obviously haven't found anyone you know. Won't I suffice?'

'But you'll be going back inside now.'

'No. The half-pricers will be in after the interval. They're a bit too rowdy for my taste.'

'I suppose it will be all right, then,' she said hesitantly.

'Good! What can I get you?'

'A port and lemon, please.'

'You don't come from this area, do you?' remarked Morton.

'How did you know that?' she smiled.

'Your vowels are a bit fuller than one gets around here.'

'I come from a little village near Stafford.' A cloud crossed her face. 'Just at this minute it seems a long way off.'

'If you'll forgive me,' ventured Morton, 'you don't sound like a village girl . . .'

'Thank you,' she laughed. 'My father was the vicar there – though I was brought up with the village children.'

'How did you find your way down here?' asked Morton, intrigued.

'Oh, I was a bit wild. I suppose I grew up too quickly.' Her smile was impish with a hint of sadness behind it. 'The boys liked me, and I didn't send them off as I should. There was one, a few years older than me, a carpenter at the boat works on the canal. He pestered me till I went out with him.'

She gazed into the ruby depths of her glass. 'Anyway, the schoolmaster caught us in what he called an "intimate embrace" behind the churchyard wall, and told my father. There was a terrible scene. My father went to see the boy's parents, and I was told that I must either marry him there and then, or leave home for good – so I married him . . . This must be very boring for you.'

'Not at all. Do go on.'

'The trouble was, neither of us wanted marriage. I'd been used to being friendly with a lot of boys, now I was stuck with one. He turned against me because he didn't want to be saddled with a wife. Least of all one who hadn't been brought up to work. After three months we were like strangers, and he was openly going about with other girls.' She leaned forward to put her glass on the counter, and her breast pressed against Morton's arm. He wished he could see her without her coat.

'Will you have another?' he asked.

'No, thank you. I ought to be getting back.'

'You haven't told me why you came down to London.'

'Oh, that's soon told! After a while he started beating me, and we couldn't stay in the village after that. He got a job with a firm in London a month ago, and we took a room in a house near here.'

'But why are you lonely?'

'I don't see much of him at the best of times, but two days ago he went to Ipswich with a barge. He said he wouldn't be back till Monday.'

Morton felt a tingle of excitement at the bottom of his spine.

'I really must go back,' she smiled.

'Then perhaps you'll let me escort you?' suggested Morton. 'It isn't particularly safe at this time of night.'

They walked cautiously along the dark street, and she held his arm tightly as if seeking reassurance. Once she missed her footing on the uneven pavement, and would have fallen had he not caught her. They stood momentarily clutching each other, without speaking, then walked on more urgently, as if some compact had been struck.

'We're there,' she said, releasing his arm. Taking a key from her purse, she half turned to go, then swung back and stood very close to him. 'Come up with me,' she said in a low voice. Without waiting for his reply, she ran up the steps and cautiously opened the door. She peered inside the dimly-lit hall, then putting a finger to her lips, beckoned him on.

He crossed the stone-flagged hallway, and found her at the bottom of the stairs. She took his hand, and they began to creep upwards. After two flights she drew him gently along a dark corridor and eased open a narrow door. The room was small and dimly lit by a street-lamp outside. The furniture was sparse and shabby. There was a bed on one side of the window, and a washing-stand and chair on the other. A small wardrobe and chest of drawers stood against the opposite wall.

She closed the door quietly behind them, and turned to him, pressing her body against his. Then she twisted away, throwing off her coat, and beginning to unbutton her dress. He stroked the silver skin of her arms as she stepped out of it, and kissed the nape of her neck while she unhooked her stays.

She turned, her breast full under her chemise. 'You're slow!' she smiled

Morton began to drag his clothes off, letting them lie where they fell.

'Now don't be untidy,' she cried, carefully folding each garment, and putting them on the chair with his boots on top. She raised the lower sash of the window a few inches, then slipped out of her chemise and into bed. The sheets were icy, and they clung together for warmth. Then relaxing, Morton began to caress her breasts.

She started to kiss him fiercely, then wrenched her head away. 'The front door!' she cried.

He raised his head and listened. Heavy, measured steps were crossing the hallway.

'Oh Christ! My husband! You've got to get out of here!'
'Are you sure?'

'Of course I'm sure! For Jesus's sake, get off of me! He'll be here in a minute,' she cried desperately. 'When he finds I'm not in the kitchen he'll come straight up!' She twisted out of bed and wriggled into a nightdress.

'But I thought he was in Ipswich.'

'So did I! For God's sake, get out of bed!'

'Are there any other stairs?' asked Morton.

'No! It'll have to be the window. There's a flat roof just under it, you'll be able to get down into the garden ... Listen! He's coming!'

Morton could hear the heavy steps re-crossing the hall, and beginning to mount the stairs. He leapt out of bed, and she thrust his clothes into his arms. Then, throwing up the sash, she bundled him on to the roof, closing and locking the window behind him.

Morton scrambled painfully to the edge of the roof, and looked back. She had lit a lamp, and was brushing her hair by the drawn blind. As he watched, another shadow crossed hers. Morton threw his clothes into the garden, and, lowering himself from the gutter, dropped after them. He quickly gathered them again, and tiptoed to the back gate. He opened it gingerly and eased himself through. Two figures were still silhouetted against the blind – all would be well! Then he let go the gate, and it swung closed with a loud screech. Morton ran in panic to the end of the alley, his clothes in his arms, then stopped and looked back. There was no sign of pursuit. He sighed with relief.

'What 'ave we 'ere then?'

Morton swung round to find a policeman regarding him with astonishment. He wondered momentarily if he should run, then decided against it. 'It's perfectly all right, officer,' he panted.

'That's as may be,' said the policeman in measured tones, 'but it ain't normal to go runnin' down the street bollock-naked in winter – 'specially when you got clothes. 'Ere,' he asked with growing interest, 'you 'aven't been indecently exposin' of yourself, 'ave you?'

'Certainly not, officer! It's just that I was visiting a lady friend and her husband came home at an inconvenient moment.'

'Before we go into that, perhaps you'll get dressed again. An' if you'll give me your boots, so you won't run off, I'll avert me eyes.'

Morton thankfully huddled on his clothes and retrieved his boots.

'Now then,' said the policeman, taking out his notebook. 'Name?'

Morton could imagine the ribald comments if this escapade got back to the City. And if Sir William heard, it might find its way to The Priory. He decided to chance his arm.

'I'm Jim Morton, the cricketer.'

'Oh yes?' said the policeman sceptically, 'I suppose you can prove that?'

'Yes, of course.' Morton felt for his pocket-book . . . but it was gone. He stupidly patted all his pockets, then went through them all again. 'I'm sorry,' he blurted, 'I seem to have lost my pocketbook.'

'P'raps you dropped it on the way from your appointment, sir.'

'No, that's not really possible. There's a flap on the pocket, and I always keep it fastened.'

'I see. Known your lady friend long, 'ave you, sir?'

'No, I picked . . . We met this evening in the bar at Harwood's Varieties.'

'Would you care to point out the house, sir?' They walked slowly down the alley, the policeman shining his lantern in each gateway.

'I think this is it,' asserted Morton. 'I could be certain if we opened the gate. It squeaked as it closed.'

'I expect they all do, sir,' observed the policeman. 'It's a thing about gates, they squeak unless they're oiled.'

'I'm sure I could identify it in the daylight.'

'This lady friend of yours. Did you 'appen to show 'er your pocket-book?'

'Well, no. But I suppose she might have seen it when I was paying the barmaid.'

'Did you 'ave much money in it, sir?'

'About fifty pounds in bank notes.'

The policeman whistled. 'I suppose she said her 'usband was away, and invited you in.'

'Yes, officer.'

'And just as you was gettin' nicely going, he comes back unexpected.'

'That's right.'

'You've been 'ad, 'aven't you, sir?'

'Yes, constable, I'm very much afraid I have.'

'One of the oldest tricks in the game! You wouldn't want to bring charges, I suppose sir?'

'No! I certainly would not!'

'Funny how they can get away with it, when they make a man look a fool, isn't it? Goodnight, sir.'

11

'Morning, sergeant,' said the uniformed constable, poking his head round the door. 'There's a young woman downstairs for you, name of Daisy Potter.'

'Bring her up, constable, will you?'

She seemed to have shrunk in size, and she looked apprehensively at the two policemen.

'Sit down, Mrs Potter. Would you like me to get you a cup of tea?'

'No, thank you.' The former remote quality in her voice had been replaced by anxiety.

'How are you getting on?' asked Bragg kindly.

'I'm managing. We're with his sister till I can find something . . . I'll have to get a job . . . but it's not easy with young children . . . ' She seemed to be withdrawing into herself again.

'And why did you come to see me?' prompted Bragg.

She opened her handbag and produced a letter. 'I got this first post this morning . . . I can't make out what it's about . . . So I thought I'd better bring it to you.' She handed the letter to Bragg. 'He's not done anything bad, has he?' she burst out, twisting her handkerchief in her fingers.

'No, nothing like that, Mrs Potter,' said Bragg reassuringly as he spread the letter on the desk so that Morton could see.

London & County Bank Ltd.,
135, Minories,
London, E.C.

28 December 1890

Dear Madam,
On the esteemed instructions of your late husband

by letter of the 1st ult., we sent the enclosed for collection. We have, however, been unable to effect collection as we understand that payment has been withheld by the drawer.

I await the favour of your instructions.

> *I am, madam,*
> *Your most obedient servant,*
> *J. Heyes*

Inside the envelope was a cheque dated 1 November, drawn in favour of A. Potter on the Crédit Lyonnais in Monte Carlo.

'I think they've just got mixed up,' observed Bragg with a smile at Mrs Potter. 'This seems like something to do with his employers. I wouldn't worry about it, if I were you. You leave it with us and forget about it. We'll see they get it.'

'Thank you, sergeant,' she said, blinking back tears. 'I knew it would be all right if I brought it to you.'

'Here,' cried Bragg, diving into his pocket and thrusting a half-sovereign on her. 'This will pay for your fares. No, you take it,' he insisted, brushing aside her protests. 'Now off you go home, and look after yourself.'

She screwed up her face in a smile, gathered her bag and gloves, and slipped out of the door.

'Well, this is a turn up!' exclaimed Bragg. 'Twenty-five thousand francs – that's a lot of money!'

'A thousand pounds, as near as makes no matter,' agreed Morton.

'Good God! Well, this is it, isn't it? Can you read the signature on that cheque? Your eyes are younger than mine.'

'It's very badly written,' said Morton, taking it to the window. 'In fact, it's just not legible at all.'

'Could it be Charles Meyers?' demanded Bragg, peering over his shoulder.

'Well, I suppose that first curve could be a C, but after that it's just a series of wiggles. I can't see an M anywhere.'

'It must be! It's the only connection with France we've

got. This is Potter's pay-out for something, and it's a hell of a lot more than a few quid. When we hear from the Marseilles police we'll get a copy of the Cross account from Meyer's books.'

'The bank must have had the cheque when I saw their ledger,' observed Morton. 'I'm sure it hadn't been credited.'

'I think that manager has some explaining to do. Come on!'

Morton followed Bragg's breakneck pace like a shooting dog kept at heel. Their path took them past the archway to French Ordinary Court, but Bragg passed it without a glance, totally preoccupied by the new situation.

The pimply youth shot a sideways look at Morton, then, in response to Bragg's peremptory demand, went to fetch the manager.

'Mr Heyes,' Bragg began forcefully, 'we are police officers, and we are enquiring into the murder of Mr Arthur Potter, who was a customer of yours.'

Heyes blinked weak eyes behind his gold-rimmed spectacles, but said nothing.

'Mrs Potter has handed us your letter of the twenty-eighth, and asked us to take any necessary action. What can you tell us about this cheque?'

'No more than's in the letter,' replied Heyes sharply.

'How did you know the drawer had stopped payment?'

'Because it said so on the covering chit from Crédit Lyonnais.'

'Why wasn't it in the ledger when we saw it a few days ago?' demanded Bragg.

'Don't you take that tone with me,' retorted Heyes angrily. 'You come into this bank in a most irregular way, you trick and bully my clerk into giving you information you are not entitled to, and now you have the effrontery to question my integrity. I won't have it!' He was trembling with fury, his clenched fists white.

Bragg dropped his voice to a threatening rumble. 'If I've got to go for a warrant, your Head Office will get to know you showed us the ledger.'

'They know already,' snapped Heyes.

'Oh no, they don't! And what's more, as soon as they find out, you'll lose your managership.'

'You tricked my clerk!'

'That won't help you. You're in charge here, you shouldn't have let it happen.'

Heyes stood sullenly, his eyes dropped to Bragg's waistcoat.

'Now, if you tell me,' said Bragg reasonably, 'I shan't need to get a warrant, and no one will be any the wiser.'

'What is it you want?' asked Heyes in a bitter voice.

'Why wasn't this cheque reflected in the account when we saw it before?'

'It's perfectly normal,' asserted Heyes. 'In the ordinary way we would have discounted the cheque and credited the proceeds within a few days. In this case Mr Potter asked for it to be sent for collection – you get a better rate that way.'

'And it took so long to go the rounds?' asked Bragg brusquely.

'Certainly – it is Christmas.'

'How did you keep track of it?'

'The covering letter and a copy of the remittance voucher are on the file.'

'Ah yes, Mr Potter's file. Can I see it?'

Heyes gave Bragg a look of concentrated malevolence, then took a slim folder from a cupboard.

'I see his employers provided a reference when he opened the account,' observed Bragg, turning over the papers.

'It's normal,' said Heyes acidly.

'This is his letter – short and to the point. Right, I don't think we shall be wanting any of these documents at the moment, sir, so I'll give you good day.'

'I've never been so abused in my life!' sputtered Heyes.

'I'm sorry you feel like that, sir,' replied Bragg heartily.

'I shall report you to your superior officer!'

'You do that, sir. Good day!'

'Proper little terrier, wasn't he?' remarked Bragg with a grin, as they walked back.

'I thought he would hit you once! Who signed the reference from Cross Shipping?'

'Our swashbuckling friend Smallshaw! Interesting, that. Do you fancy him being in on it?'

'I can't imagine it,' replied Morton. 'He seems afraid of his own shadow.'

'You can see why they needed a bank account, though, and it isn't all that easy for the indigent to open one. It will bear thinking about.'

'Any messages?' asked Bragg of the duty sergeant.

'None for you, Joe, but we had a telephone message for Detective Constable Morton.' The sergeant articulated every syllable with care. 'From his stockbrokers no less. It seems they want him to go round. They say it's a matter of extreme importance.'

'I'd better go,' said Morton in embarrassment. 'I'll be straight back.'

'Ah, James! Enter the holy of holies!' cried Denton. 'Will you have a pre-prandial sherry?'

'I'd be glad to,' laughed Morton. 'I've just witnessed a poor bank manager being browbeaten by my sergeant. A sherry might steady my nerves!'

'Tut, tut! Can't have you running amok among the professional classes.'

'I suppose it was necessary, but I'd never be able to bring it off.'

'Up the ladies,' said Denton absently. 'Oh, by the way, thank you for the invitation.'

'Ah, mother wrote to you then? Good!'

'On the last stroke of Christmas. I am summoned for the weekend beginning the first of February.'

'I'll do my best to be there.'

'I'd prefer it if you'd do your best not to be there . . . so that I can have . . . ' he licked his lips wickedly – 'the lovely Lady Ermintrude . . . in my powah!'

'I think you're half serious,' laughed Morton.

'Ah James, you deceive yourself . . . I'm all serious –

about the money. Which brings us back to our muttons. Don't!'

'Don't what?'

'The worthy Cross. Don't!'

'Why?'

'I've sounded out the old contacts, and had a word with pater, and we think he's a bad risk.'

'Really?' exclaimed Morton.

'Cross Shipping is an old-established firm, one of the pillars of the City. Sir Charles has been Lord Mayor – as was his father before him. Still, I doubt whether his word is his bond anymore.'

'How's that?'

'In his father's day they were very prosperous. Nothing big, a lot of coastal trade, shipping as far as the Med and down the west coast of Africa. All sail in those days. Then came steam, and they got left behind. When young Sir Charles took the helm, he couldn't bear that. So, he decided to break in with the big boys. It was the time when they begin shipping frozen meat from Australia. Sir Charles spent a fortune on a new refrigerated ship – the *Southern Cross*, you may have heard of her – and he sent his merry men off to bring home the bacon!'

'Behave yourself!' exclaimed Morton, then realized with amusement that it was one of Bella's admonishments.

'Of course by this time,' Denton went on, 'the big boys had it all sewn up, and they didn't want him joining their club. So they simply dropped their rates.'

'What does that mean?'

'Their freight rates. They had the trade parcelled out between them, and Cross hadn't a hope of filling his ship anyway. When they dropped their rate-per-ton, it meant that to compete he had to run at a disastrous loss.'

'I see.'

'He kept it up for eighteen months, by which time all their profits had taken a beating, so they let him in. He got his heart's desire, but they ruined him in the process.'

'So he's not a wealthy man at all?' asked Morton.

'It depends on how you measure it. In terms of disposable cash, certainly not. I'm going to tell you something now that's not generally known even in our trade, so I'd be grateful if you'd keep it under that nauseating billycock you affect!'

Denton dropped his voice conspiratorially. 'The other members of the Conference crucified him, as I've said, and then there was all that trouble with the new docks at Tilbury, so that a couple of years ago our good Sir Charles was all but finished. So off he goes to the bank for a loan. They turn him down! He goes on his knees to them. "Pity my poor orphans!" he says. So they relent. But they won't give him a straight loan, they want a slice of the dynamic new era. They force him to float a company to take over the business, and they subscribe for forty per cent of the equity.'

'So what happened to the money the bank paid out for its shares?'

Denton laid a finger along his nose. 'All tied up in the business, my boy.'

'Are you telling me he only owns sixty per cent of Cross Shipping?' asked Morton excitedly.

'I am telling you that, O sharer of my chamber pot!'

'You've trumped my ace, damn you!' cried Bragg in huge delight. 'I got this telegram from Marseilles, not ten minutes after we got back. I'm told this incomprehensible frog lingo means that there's no coaling agent in Marseilles by the name of Charles Meyer.'

Morton took the telegram and perused it.

'That means,' Bragg went on gleefully, 'that the Meyer account is a fabrication. And who told us it was genuine? None other than our respected ex-Lord Mayor, Sir Charles Cross!'

'Do you think he fabricated it?' asked Morton.

'Why not? You've just supplied us with a cast-iron motive. Much better to get a hundred per cent in your pocket, than sixty percent locked up in a company – particularly if you're broke!'

'I can't believe he's as broke as all that,' protested Morton. 'How could he afford to run an enormous yacht like the *Athena*, if he were?'

'Don't be naïve, lad, it'll be down to the company – won't cost him a penny. I think it's time we asked our friend Cross a serious question or two!'

'Come on!' mimicked Morton with a grin.

'Sir Charles?' smiled the young woman. 'No, I'm afraid he's on holiday.'

'Holiday?' echoed Bragg, dumbfounded.

'Yes, he's gone to France.'

'When?'

'Last night.'

'Do you know where he went?'

'No, he didn't say.'

'Did he get his ticket through a railway agent?'

'No, he said he'd buy it at Victoria.'

'I suppose he didn't leave a forwarding address?' asked Bragg disconsolately.

'No. He said he'd cable us . . . Sorry!'

Bragg called a hansom and sat fuming with impatience at every check until they reached the docks. Before the cab had stopped he was dashing towards the office of Cross Shipping. He rapped on the counter for attention. 'Mr Green, please,' he called.

'He's not in,' replied the gangling youth who had emerged from the shadowy depths of the store.

'Find out where he is, will you?'

'Wait a minute.'

Bragg chewed his moustache and watched with narrowed eyes as the youth returned.

'You've only just missed him,' he said. 'He left for Dover twenty minutes ago to catch the Ostend packet.'

'When will he be back?' asked Bragg urgently.

'Jim!' called the youth. 'When will Lofty be back?'

'It doesn't matter!' cried Bragg as he sprinted for the door. 'Cabby, get us to the nearest telegraph office, quick as you can!' He grinned fiercely at Morton. 'Something tells me our luck is turning. I'm going to telegraph a description of Green to the Dover police. We ought to have him in the bag before the night's out.'

12

'Hello, Bragg,' cried Inspector Davis. 'Don't see much of you nowadays. Going to see the big white chief?'

Bragg nodded, and sat down beside him on one of the bentwood chairs that graced the ante-room of the Commissioner's office.

'What are you on then?' asked Davis, tenderly smoothing his luxuriant brown whiskers with the back of his fingers.

'The carpet, I expect,' replied Bragg shortly.

Davis raised an enquiring eyebrow, but Bragg would not be drawn.

'You've got young Silver Morton, haven't you?' enquired Davis.

'Silver?'

'You know, silver spoon! How's he getting on?'

'Well enough, though it's early days yet.'

'I had him in the sixth division. I must say we had a few laughs out of him. The second or third time he was on point duty – outside the Baltic it was – a young woman comes up to him and asks him to help her get a cab. Spun him some yarn about her mother being sick. He sees one discharging in Threadneedle Street, so he holds up the traffic and beckons it over. By the time it comes, there's a hell of a tangle, buses and vans and carts all over the place. Not that it worries Silver! He hands the lady up, touches his helmet to her and waves the cab on – then starts trying to sort out the mess. And all the time,' chuckled Davis, 'and all the time her old man is doing a smash and grab on the silversmith's round the corner! That was a laugh that was!' He gently stroked his moustache in case his mirth had misplaced a hair. 'Mind you, he made up for it. He's pretty lively with a pencil, is Silver, and he made us a sketch of the woman. We could see straight away it was Nifty Larkin's judy. Picked 'em up with no trouble at all – swag still under the bed!'

'He's maturing nicely,' remarked Bragg. 'We're about to hang a man because he didn't take the band off his cigar!'

'Ah well, we could do worse.'

'How do you mean?'

'Surely you've heard the rumour?'

'What rumour?' asked Bragg sharply.

'They do say he's to be the next Commissioner.'

'The next Commissioner?' repeated Bragg incredulously.

'Work it out for yourself, sergeant. Sir William has about fifteen years to do. Young Silver will be forty then. Just the right age according to some people's notions.'

'But why?' demanded Bragg.

'They say the Home Secretary wants us to grow our own, instead of taking someone from the Army. It seems the military approach is out of fashion after the Trafalgar Square riots.'

'God Almighty! It's enough to make me vote Liberal!'

'Steady on, sergeant! In a couple of years, he'll be your boss!'

'Let me remind you that you're investigating the death of this man Potter,' said Sir William testily, 'and not imaginary delinquencies of Sir Charles Cross.'

Lieutenant-Colonel Sir William Sumner was a short stiff man, who ran the force in the paternalistic way he had run his regiment. With fewer than eight hundred men under him, his personal influence reached down to the rawest constable on the beat. Born a few years before the Prince of Wales, he affected the same close-cropped hair and pointed beard, so that there was a pronounced – some said carefully cultivated – resemblance between them.

'In my view, sir,' replied Bragg unemphatically, 'the evidence shows that Sir Charles is involved in activities which are almost certainly criminal.'

'We'll come to that,' retorted Sir William. 'But let's be clear on one thing. Before we start making allegations about respected City figures, we've got to be very sure of our ground. Damn it, he's not an upstart! His family have been in the City for generations, he's an ex-Lord Mayor and an Alderman. He has a great deal of influence in the City, and a reputation that's absolutely unblemished. I will not allow a criminal charge to be brought against someone like that without being satisfied we shall secure a conviction. Understand?'

'Yes, sir.'

'I've read your report, and discussed it with Chief Inspector Forbes here, and it seems to me we aren't justified in asking for extradition. I know I'm still something of an amateur in these matters, but from what I can see the evidence points to Potter as the wrong 'un, not Cross.'

'Potter is hardly likely to have engineered his own death,' remarked Bragg.

'But your submission is built on the assumption that the . . . the inconsistencies in the books of Cross Shipping are connected with Potter's death. I don't see why it's necessary to make the connection. It could just as easily have been a casual footpadding.'

'On the evidence, sir, I don't think we are justified in treating them as unconnected,' said Bragg. 'It's beyond doubt that Potter took the cheque to the bank as soon as he left the office, and he was murdered on the way back.'

'That's no reason to decide that he was murdered because of the cheque,' interposed Forbes. He had big white teeth under a waxed moustache, and liked to smile often. 'You say it was a crossed cheque, so the would-be thief couldn't have cashed it anyway.'

'The murderer might not have known that.'

'I don't like the word "murder" being bandied about,' complained Sir William. 'Surely we're making an unwarranted assumption.'

'Not if Dr. Burney's report is to be believed,' replied Bragg.

'What reliance can be placed on it, Forbes?'

The Chief Inspector moved uncomfortably in his chair. 'I

think,' he said cautiously, 'that we should give great weight to his opinion.'

Sir William looked sharply at him, then back to Bragg. 'All right, so it was murder. Nevertheless, I won't have you subjecting Sir Charles to a murder enquiry without definite evidence.'

'The evidence we have clearly suggests that Cross may be implicated,' said Bragg evenly.

'You would need more to secure a conviction,' observed Forbes.

'We would need answers to a few questions, yes,' agreed Bragg. 'Which is why we should extradite him from France.'

'It's all too premature,' exclaimed Sir William. 'We don't even know he's fled the country. Plenty of people go to the continent at this time of year.'

'Our information indicates that he has, sir.'

'You're putting altogether too much reliance on gossip from the mistress, Bragg,' remarked Forbes.

'That indeed may be the case, sir,' agreed Bragg with studied mildness. 'Though since you have read my report, you will realize there are independent reasons for suspicion.'

Sir William interrupted hastily. 'What exactly are you suggesting Cross has done?' he asked.

'I'm saying he defrauded the company by transferring money abroad against fictitious purchases. I'm saying that Potter found out and blackmailed Cross, who had him killed by Lofty Green.'

'Why take the ledger account and invoices?' asked Forbes.

'To conceal the fraud.'

'It would merely serve to draw attention to it,' countered Forbes.

'Only if it was investigated by someone who knew what they were looking for.'

'So who took them?' asked Sir William.

'On my analysis, Cross took them,' replied Bragg.

'I doubt if he would know enough about the books to find what he was looking for,' objected Forbes.

'You make my point for me, sir,' observed Bragg reasonably. 'Once you accept they were destroyed to conceal something – and you must – then it can't have been Potter who did it. Potter was dealing with these records every day. He would have been more selective, he'd have taken only the Meyer invoices and paid cheques. More important, he'd have destroyed the Day Book as well. I doubt if Cross even knew it existed.'

'What about Smallshaw?' asked Sir William. 'He seems to have been involved with Potter's bank account.'

'He's much too timid to be trusted in anything dishonest,' said Bragg. 'From what Green said, he was bullied by Cross until he would do anything he was told, without question.'

'But he could have destroyed the vouchers.'

'He could, Sir William, but the same objections apply to him as apply to Potter. In my book, the only person who destroyed those documents was Sir Charles Cross.'

'It would be possible to argue that it was Potter,' intervened Forbes, 'if one accepted that he only wanted to conceal his misdeeds for a short period. He might, for instance, have decided to leave his employment. It would have served long enough for that, wouldn't it, Bragg?'

'It would, sir, but there's no indication that he intended to leave his job.'

'I would have thought you could have assumed that he would,' said Forbes with heavy sarcasm. 'After all, you found it possible to assume that Potter had been blackmailing Cross. Surely to God you didn't expect them to work together harmoniously for the rest of time!'

'We're getting away from the point,' said Sir William peremptorily. 'I take it, Bragg, that you do accept Potter was a wrong 'un?'

'In view of the cheque, and his deliberate murder, I must do so, sir.'

'Why couldn't the cheque have come from other criminal activities?'

'It is possible, but I feel it's unlikely. After all, it's a very large sum.'

'This is where you are going wrong,' broke in Forbes. 'You are trying to force the Meyer account and the Potter killing into one pattern, against the evidence. You ought to forget the fraud and concentrate on the murder.'

'I'm sure you're not suggesting,' rejoined Bragg evenly, 'that we should ignore the evidence of a possible fraud by Sir Charles Cross, merely because we discovered it while investigating something else.'

Forbes's face reddened. 'You know damned well what I mean.'

'I agree that you may be assuming a connection that doesn't exist, Bragg,' observed Sir William. 'To me it seems more likely that Potter and Green were working some fraud through the Crowe and Scrutton account, and that Green killed Potter to get all the proceeds himself.'

'That would be possible,' replied Bragg. 'Indeed I can't prove it wasn't going on. But the cheque was far too big for that – and anyway Green would have known it wasn't negotiable.'

'You haven't even proved that Green was the killer yet,' said Forbes critically.

'No, but I shall.'

Sir William pulled a sheet of paper towards him, and selected a pencil from the silver inkstand on his deck. 'Let's go to the evidence against Cross,' he suggested, 'without all this conjecture.'

'First of all,' began Bragg, 'the sale of the shares to the bank a couple of years ago gave him the motive, and it ties up roughly with the opening of the Meyer account.'

'That's not evidence,' interjected Forbes. 'Not everyone with a motive stoops to crime, mercifully.'

Bragg ignored the interruption. 'Then when we look at the Meyer account, we find large sums have been paid out that Cross must have known about, because he signed the cheques. When we questioned him about Meyer, he said he was a perfectly reputable bunkering-agent in Marseilles. We contact a foreign coaling-agent in London, and he hasn't heard of Meyer. We cable the Marseilles police, and they can't find any trace of him.'

'I think you place too much weight on the French police report,' said Forbes portentously. 'Even if Meyer doesn't exist as such, it's quite possible that the transactions in that account are genuine. He could have done business with a Marseilles coaling-agent, and put them through in the name of Meyer because the Frenchman asked him to.'

'As to the murder of Potter, the man with the best reason for getting rid of him was Cross,' went on Bragg doggedly. 'And we shouldn't forget Ramshorn. Not many people knew we had him, or that he would be taken to Mincing Lane to be charged. Sir Charles, as a magistrate, was in a position to discover both these things.'

'Can you prove he did?' asked Forbes.

'No. But we know he had lunch with John Fredericks on the Sunday Ramshorn was sprung, and Fredericks was due to hear the committal proceedings next morning.'

'It all depends on assumptions that could be unwarranted,' observed Forbes judicially. 'First the theory that the Meyer account is fraudulent, then that Potter blackmailed Cross, and, most far-fetched of all, that Cross would involve a third party to procure Potter's murder.'

'We needn't go any further,' declared Sir William. 'We must have a prima facie case before asking the Home Office to start extradition proceedings, and quite clearly we haven't got it. Your request is refused, Bragg.'

'In that case, sir, I would like your permission to go to France and question Cross.'

'What do you want to do that for?' asked Sir William.

'So far as I am aware,' said Bragg evenly, 'a man isn't exempt from being questioned about a crime merely because he's been Lord Mayor of London.'

Sir William flushed. 'Dammit, Bragg,' he exclaimed angrily. 'You're being impertinent! I meant, why can't you wait till he gets back before questioning him?'

'My belief that he's not coming back isn't based only on

what Bella Berkeley said. You'll remember that Cross's yacht did sail from London, a couple of days before he went to France. We shall look very silly if he's taken a train to St Nazaire and sailed off into the blue.'

'How do you propose to find him? asked Sir William.

'We'll keep track of his yacht from here, through Lloyd's,' said Bragg, 'I'll go to Marseilles and try to find him from the Meyer end.'

'What about your other cases?'

'They won't spoil.'

'Very well,' said Sir William grudgingly. 'You may go for that limited purpose only. And understand, you are not to make any allegations against Sir Charles Cross without my express authority.'

'I understand, sir. May I take Constable Morton with me? He speaks French far better than I do.'

'That hardly seems necessary,' remarked Forbes crushingly. 'The expenses of the detective division are too high already.'

'Very good, sir.'

'By the way, Bragg,' said Sir William, crumpling his piece of paper into a ball. 'How is Morton coming along . . . ?'

'That doesn't sound like Sir William,' exclaimed Morton. 'Whatever can have induced him to take that attitude?'

'A man isn't always as impressive on the job as he seems when you meet him socially,' replied Bragg sardonically. 'It's perfectly simple, he's afraid for his job.'

'Afraid for his job?' echoed Morton in surprise.

'You should read the bits of the Police Act that aren't printed at the back of the regulations. You'd see in section three that the Lord Mayor and Aldermen can sack the Commissioner on their say so. "For misconduct or any other reasonable cause" is the phrase. No Commissioner would last long who allowed his flatfoots to go around accusing Aldermen of fraud and murder.'

'So we're up against political pressure?'

'If you like, lad. Get in among the nobs, and they close ranks on you.'

'But that's intolerable!' exclaimed Morton.

'I thought you might find that interesting.' Bragg scanned Morton's face, but he showed no reaction to the innuendo.

'Why wouldn't they let me go with you?' asked Morton.

'Partly Forbes being the bloody-minded pig he is, and partly because they hope that without someone who speaks French, I shan't get anywhere.'

'I got you Meyer's address from the woman at Cross Shipping,' said Morton, 'Fortunately she knew it off by heart.'

'Good lad! What is it?'

'Fifty-seven, Rue Vacon, Marseilles.'

'Right then, I'll catch the next boat-train.'

'Did they positively say I mustn't go?' asked Morton.

'No. Forbes just said it was an unnecessary expense.'

'Well then,' grinned Morton, 'I have some leave left, I can't think of anything better than a few days in Marseilles!'

'He's a rough lad, this one,' remarked the constable as they followed him down the green-painted passage of the new police station at Dover. 'It took three of us to get the darbies on him.'

'You'd better stay around then, in case he tries anything,' remarked Bragg.

'He already has,' chuckled the constable. 'Foxing sleep this morning when they took his grub in. Lucky there were two of 'em.' He unlocked the cell door.

'Well now, Lofty,' remarked Bragg genially. 'Skipping the country, were you?'

'No, I bleeding wasn't,' cried Green truculently. 'I was off to our agents at Ostend when the bloody rozzers jumped me. What the hell is this about?"

'You seem to have been a bit more agitated than an innocent man would be in the circumstances,' observed Bragg, perching himself on the narrow bunk and taking out his pipe.

'I ain't done nothing. You've no right to jug me.'

'Now then, Lofty,' admonished Bragg. 'No need to get abusive. We just wanted to ask you a few questions.'

'I answered all your bleedin' questions.'

'What d'you knock off old Joe Ramshorn for? Were you told to?'

'What are you on about? I don't know any Joe Ramshorn.'

'Yes, you do,' remarked Bragg amiably. 'You sprung him from Mincing Lane, then tapped him one and put him in the river. The duty-sergeant gave us a very good description of you.'

'Bleedin' liar!'

'You coshed him one, just like you did to Potter that night in French Ordinary. And the constable in the nick. He got a good look at you too. You might as well admit it.'

'I ain't saying nothin'.'

'Of course we know you didn't kill Potter over the little fiddle with Crowe and Scrutton. It was over something much bigger, wasn't it? Why don't you tell us about it? I might be able to bring it off as manslaughter.'

'Leave me be!'

'We knew you'd move as soon as we mentioned the Meyer account. And you fell for it – Cross as well. Did he tip you off?'

Green spat derisively on the floor.

'You're a fool, Lofty. Cross will let you swing for it. He'll come out bright and shining, and all the shit will stick to you . . . We know he got you to rub out Potter and Ramshorn, but you won't be able to prove a thing. Now if you give us the story we might be able to help.'

'I've told you,' snarled Green. 'I'm saying fuck-all to you.'

'Very well,' said Bragg, turning to the constable. 'I want him taken under guard to Mincing Lane Station, and charged with the murders of Arthur Potter and Joseph Ramshorn. And tell them to make sure that Constable Preston has a good look at him.'

13

The Channel crossing had been rough. Bragg and Morton, unable to obtain a cabin, had huddled themselves into chairs in the saloon and tried to sleep. Snow had fallen heavily in Paris, turning the streets into a confused tangle of slithering vehicles and frightened horses. At Bragg's insistence they walked to the Gare de Lyon, holding on to railings and picking their way along the icy pavements. In the Place de la République a pair of van horses had been brought down by the ice. One had evidently broken its leg and was screaming hideously. The other was trying to get up, plunging and scrabbling futilely against the weight of its companion. Around them a gesticulating knot of carmen and passers-by had gathered, while a harassed policeman waved his baton and blew his whistle in an attempt to keep the other traffic moving.

They arrived at the station to find that the lines south of Paris had been blocked by snow, and were not expected to be cleared for some hours. Leaving the milling crowds, they found a brasserie in a quiet side-street and ordered a late breakfast.

Bragg's heart sank on seeing the greasy croissants, and he watched sourly as Morton zestfully broke one and dipped it in his coffee. He began to feel that the trip was doomed, a fatuous waste of time. Even the weather was conspiring to keep Cross out of his reach. Not that he would envy him if he were on the Atlantic. The gale had threatened to work up into a storm, and big as the *Athena* might be, she was no Cunarder. What a fool he would look if he came back empty-handed! Cotton would be airily sympathetic, though he'd never really backed him; Forbes would complain about the waste of time and money – and they'd all be laughing behind their whiskers. They'd only let him go because they knew he'd fail. And here he was, sitting in the corner of a freezing frog café, watching Morton reading Zola because he needed to brush up his French – or so he said. He wondered dejectedly why he bothered to fight them. He certainly got thanks from no one for it. If he'd been prepared to accept that Potter had been killed by an over-enthusiastic footpad, everybody would have been happy. Cotton had suggested as much – not that he'd known about Cross, it was just the accepted attitude: 'One of the masses? Well, get rid of it! Don't waste your time!' That was the way to get on all right, it had taken Forbes right to the top. Look keen, don't step out of line, remember who pays the rates!

Bragg looked across the table at Morton, absorbed in his book. That was a funny business. If Davis was right, Morton hadn't shown any sign of it. Not that he would, he could roast you rotten and keep as serious as a judge. There must be something in it, though, he wouldn't be in the force otherwise; and yet he'd decided to come to France without a second thought. That wouldn't go down well with Sir William, if it ever came out. But Morton wouldn't care, he had the old aristocratic outlook. Perhaps he would make a good Commissioner, somebody from the top of the pile for once. Maybe that was the trouble with Sumner, starting in the middle and rising through favour. Perhaps he'd determined that his successor wouldn't be open to manipulation by City interests as he was. Someone like Morton wouldn't dream of bending to such pressures.

But if such a plan was to succeed, Morton would have to seem the inevitable choice. He'd have to keep his nose clean, particularly in the early years. Bragg realized with mortification that he should not have allowed Morton to come. His immediate reaction had been that Morton had found the scent a couple of times, and that if he wanted, he'd every right to be in at the death. But was the truth more that he was using Morton to hit back at Sumner and Forbes? Or even more disquieting, that he was becoming dependent on

Morton? He shied away from the thought. 'Come on, lad, let's stretch our legs and see if it's thawing yet.'

The sky had cleared as darkness fell, and the full moon turned the landscape into an arctic waste. The lights from the dining-car scurried along the track beside them, bounding over snowdrifts and culverts, hiding the scrub and leaping back with them into the tunnels.

They had been forced to take berths on the evening *train de luxe*. Bragg had been horrified at the cost, and irritated at the easy opening it would give to Forbes. But after a couple of whiskies he felt warm and pleasantly tired. Once dinner was over he would turn in, try to catch up on some sleep.

'You'll have to help me with the menu, lad,' he said. 'My French isn't up to this sort of thing.'

'On the right you'll find the set meal,' said Morton, 'and the à la carte on the left.'

'Thirty-five francs! That seems a great deal for six courses. Perhaps I ought to try the left ... Hey! Look under the hors d'oeuvres, the pâté is twenty-two francs on its own! That would look fine on my expenses claim! I'll stick to the set meal. Let's see. "Potage paysanne" – that's countryside, isn't it?'

'It'll be a thick vegetable soup.'

'Just the ticket for a night like this. What's the next one: "Grenouilles aux persil"?'

'I'm afraid I can't tell you. I'm fairly sure that "persil" is parsley.'

'Ah well, I'm game for anything. "Bifteck marchand de vin", what's that?'

'I would say it's steak cooked in a wine sauce, wouldn't you?'

'Sounds fine to me. I doubt if I'll get any further. What are you having?'

'Oh, I'll have the same – and perhaps you'll join me in a bottle of wine?'

'I will that! You know, this is rather special for me,'

confided Bragg. 'Mrs Jenks is all right as a cook, but steak
and kidney pudding and spotted dick gets a bit boring. It'll
have been worth this trip if we get nothing out of it but the
food. I suppose you get this kind of thing fairly often?'

'Only when I go to Rules or the Savoy. We have plain
English cooking at The Priory.'

'The what?'

'Ashwell Priory – my parents' home.'

'Thank God! I thought we were turning you into a monk,'
laughed Bragg. 'I should have known better. You know,' he
continued, 'I still can't understand you being in the police. A
background among the landed aristocracy, wealthy family,
plenty of friends – everything a young man could want. And
instead you flat-foot it round the City for two years like any
country numbskull.'

'Perhaps it's a measure of my failure, sergeant,' said
Morton, pushing away his soup plate, and dabbing fastidi-
ously at his mouth with a napkin.

'Meaning what?'

'One can be rich without effort, to be idle as well requires
considerable dedication. I was no good at it.'

'Oh, very witty!'

'It's true,' Morton assured him. 'I'm not cut out for a
society life. I like riding and boating and cricket, but I
prefer to take part, not just watch. Moreover, I don't relish
the prospect of being hunted by predatory mothers and
acquisitive girls. For me the police force is a perfect escape.
I'm safe!'

'You'll never get away,' laughed Bragg. 'In a couple of
years your mother will start turning on the pressure and
you'll be finished. Once she goes over to the enemy, you
might as well surrender.'

'When I marry, I at least intend to choose the girl myself.'

'Good luck to you! Here, these grenouilles things look
funny . . .'

'And what about you, sergeant?' asked Morton quickly.

'How do you mean?'

'Well, you're far from the ordinary type of policeman

yourself. You're cultured and well-read, you have a wide experience of life and a deep understanding of people . . . '

'Oh, I don't know about that,' protested Bragg, sunning himself in the compliments.

'Why did you become a policeman?'

'It's a long story, lad . . . These things have got bones in them – taste good though, a bit like chicken.'

'We've plenty of time,' prompted Morton.

'Well, in my teens I was working in a shipping office in Weymouth – a branch of a London firm. By the time I was seventeen I was practically running it . . . I think these things are the wings of some bird, grenouille sounds like something that flies . . . Anyway, the boss came down from London one day, and offered me the chance of working at Head Office. Of course I jumped at it. Poor old mum! You'd have thought I was going to the north pole, the way she went on. It was interesting being in a big office, but it wasn't as much fun as Weymouth, where I was doing a bit of everything. After a couple of years I couldn't see my way forward, and I was getting a bit restless. Then one night I was in a dockside pub when a bit of a fight started. The landlord yelled blue murder, and in came the local copper to sort it out. Of course, they all went for him; poor bugger was getting belted from every side. So I gave him a bit of a hand. After that we became real friends – John Cavanagh, big Irishman, solid as a rock. Keeps a pub now in Stoke Newington. I suppose it was him that decided me to join the police – and the chance of one of the married quarters in Bishopsgate. I'd been courting a girl from Briantspuddle for some time. At long range as you might say. I reckoned that would just about clinch it . . . ' He pushed away his plate and polished his ragged moustache on his napkin. 'I don't know when I enjoyed anything as much. We must find out what they are.'

Inspector Forestier met them at Marseilles with a roomy pony-chaise that he said was his official vehicle. He was swarthy and voluble, and as he spoke he would purse his lips and twist his mouth as if he had to give physical birth to every word. As Bragg had obviously given up trying to follow the conversation, Morton outlined their plans to the Frenchman. They clattered down the avenue from the station and were soon swallowed up in the narrow streets around the Old Port. Although they had left the snow behind them at Avignon, a cold wind blew from the east, sending the dead leaves swirling, and stinging their faces with grains of sand.

'It is there,' cried Forestier, reining in and pointing with his whip.

'Where?' asked Morton.

They had stopped by a row of shabby shops, with peeling paint, and broken shutters groaning in the wind.

'Between the grocery and the horse-butcher.'

In a recess was a door, its foot scarred by many boots, the knob hanging drunkenly. The number was just discernible above it. They pushed inside, and Forestier led the way up a flight of steep wooden stairs to the quarters above. He rapped on the door with a flourish.

'Who is there?' called a quavering voice.

'Police!'

'A moment.'

There came the rattle of a chain and the squeal of a key in the lock. Then the door was opened a crack and a single yellowing eye inspected them. Forestier waved his identification card, and the door was shut again while the chain was released.

'Come in, gentlemen.' He was old and stooping, his soiled shirt collarless. 'How can I help you?' he asked.

'You have received letters from England,' cried Forestier fiercely. 'What have you done with them?'

'I do not understand.'

'They contained cheques from Cross Shipping Company in London,' said Morton.

'I have seen no cheques,' protested the old man.

'They were addressed to Charles Meyer, here,' cried Forestier.

'I know nothing about them.'

Forestier seized him by the neck-band and forced him upright. 'My friend,' he said softly, 'a man has been killed – an Englishman. They have come from London to take you back with them. If you persist in denying, I shall allow it, and you can spend the rest of your miserable life in an English prison. Tell me!' he roared, flinging the man across the room on to a ramshackle settee.

'Tell me!' He advanced threateningly, and the old man raised a defensive arm.

'It is nothing,' he whined. 'I used to receive letters addressed to Charles Meyer. According to my instructions I would put the letter unopened into an envelope, and send it to an address in Lyon.'

'What address?' demanded Forestier.

The man rose apprehensively, and went into the next room. After a few moments he came back carrying a crumpled piece of paper. 'Maître Rochat,' he read, 'forty-two Place Bellecour, Lyon.'

'How were you paid for this?' asked Morton.

'I would receive a sum from Maître Rochat each month.'

Forestier raised his eyebrows questioningly.

'Did you follow all that?' asked Morton.

'Enough,' replied Bragg heavily. 'It's us for the next train to Lyon. That's another bloody day wasted!'

The Lyon police provided an inspector and a sergeant, though Bragg could not decide whether it was out of respect for him, or deference to Maître Rochat. Morton introduced himself, and Rochat held out his hand with a charming smile.

'I am enchanted to make your acquaintance,' he said in English. 'I do not often have the honour of entertaining the English police.' He motioned them to plump chairs with a hospitable wave of the hand.

'We are making enquiries about some letters which have been sent to you,' began Bragg. 'Letters addressed to Charles Meyer.'

'From whom did you obtain the information that letters were sent here?' asked Rochat.

'An old man in Rue Vacon, Marseilles.'

'And what did he say about the letters?'

'That he received them from England, put them unopened into another envelope, and sent them to you.'

'A very strange story. What could be the reason for such a subterfuge, I wonder?'

'To conceal a fraud on an English company.'

'An English company,' mused Rochat. 'There has been a crime in England in connection with the letters you tell me about?'

'Yes.'

'You can prove it?'

'Yes,' asserted Bragg defiantly. 'And what's more, a man has been murdered.'

'In connection with the letters?' asked Rochat.

'Yes.'

'In England?'

'Yes.'

Rochat leaned back in his chair, locked his hands behind his head, and stared at the ceiling. Then he crossed to a bookcase, took down a volume, and turned quickly through the pages. 'Ah, *oui*,' he murmured, bringing it back to his desk. 'These crimes have not been committed on the soil of France,' he observed pleasantly, 'so why do you come to me?'

'Because we have reason to believe that the perpetrator of them is now in France,' replied Bragg.

'But, m'sieur, both these crimes are embraced by the treaty of extradition between our countries. Why approach me in this way?'

'Because we don't know where he is, so he can't be arrested. Secondly we believe that he is going to leave France within a few days.'

'It would seem,' remarked Rochat, scrutinizing the nails of his left hand minutely, 'that the law is not effective in your aid. And unfortunately I am unable to help you. Even if the story of this old man were true – which I do not admit – you have shown me no reason why I should breach the professional confidence that would be between me and my client – if such a client existed.'

He rose from his chair and walked briskly to the door. 'Good morning, gentlemen,' he said, shaking Bragg and Morton punctiliously by the hand.

'They're all the same, lawyers,' said Bragg bitterly, when they were alone on the pavement. 'Whatever country they're in, if you want an answer from them, you've got to be able to tell them what it is, and prove to them that they know it, before they'll let on.'

'What do we do now?' asked Morton.

'Charles Meyer's a dead duck, that's for certain. So we've only got the bank account left. What time's the next train to Monte Carlo, lad?'

14

They left their bags at the station and took an open carriage to the Hôtel de Ville. Although it had two horses, Morton began to wonder if they would manage the steep pull up the hairpin road to Monaco.

'Spectacular, isn't it?' observed Bragg, looking back over the harbour with its scattering of white yachts and steamers moored to seaward. 'Like a picture, with those rugged hills coming right down to the sea, and Monte Carlo clinging to the bottom.'

'And to think that thirty years ago there wasn't a building there.'

'The lure of easy wealth, my boy!'

'Do you fancy a spin at the Casino, sergeant?'

'Not me, lad, I've more sense than to throw away my hard-earned money.'

'Expenses?' suggested Morton. 'Surely they'd stretch to that? Put it down as cab fares.'

'I bet you bloody would, too. Let me remind you that Potter got the chop for something not much worse than that. Ah, we seem to be getting somewhere at last.'

They breasted the rise, and rattled into a street bordered by tall stucco buildings, with balconies on the lower floors. Their terracotta and orange walls turned the shadowed street into the floor of a canyon. The awnings of the shops projected so far into the carriageway that their driver was sometimes forced to bend his head to avoid them. They skirted the cathedral, and pulled up by an imposing stone building with a semi-circular front. Two balustraded stair-cases curved towards a central portal on the first floor, emblazoned with the arms of Grimaldi. Above, an ornamental battlement broke the tiled eaves, and from it the red and

159

white diamonds fluttered in the breeze. Bragg started up one staircase and, whimsically, Morton took the other. They arrived at the top together, and turned inwards to the door simultaneously.

'We ought to do a turn at the Empire,' remarked Bragg with a smile. 'Something tells me that after this lot we shall have to.'

Inspector Doriot received them without warmth, and as their story unfolded his lugubrious face drooped until he resembled an old St Bernard. 'But messieurs,' he said in his halting English, 'I do not understand how you make the connection between this Charles Meyer and the bank account here in Monte Carlo.'

'I believe that the cheques paid by Cross Shipping are sent here by the lawyer in Lyon,' said Bragg.

'And you say this Sir Charles Cross controls it all?'

'That's right.'

'But if that is correct, why should he pay the murdered man by a cheque on the Monte Carlo account? Evidently he would have funds in England for this purpose.'

'He didn't pay him, did he?' retorted Bragg. 'Payment was stopped.'

Doriot steepled his long fingers and rested his chin on them. 'You are saying,' he observed to the sunlit wall of the cathedral, 'that he gave him a Crédit Lyonnais cheque so that he could have time to provide for his murder?'

'Perhaps,' replied Bragg. 'We don't know whether instructions were sent to stop the cheque before Potter was murdered, or after. We shall find out when we see the bank manager here.'

'And you wish me to do what?' asked Doriot.

'I would like you to come with us,' said Bragg uncomfortably, 'to persuade him to give us the information we need to arrest Cross.'

Before Bragg finished, Doriot was swivelling his head on the points of his fingers. 'It is not possible,' he said dolefully. 'I cannot believe in this connection between Charles Meyer and the bank account here. As for the murder ... ' he shrugged his shoulders dismissively.

'We need to question him to establish the connection,' urged Bragg.

'And if he will not answer?' asked Doriot. 'I cannot force him to answer without a warrant from the court, and even if you had evidence it would take time.'

'How long?'

'To be truthful, m'sieur, since an Englishman is concerned, I doubt if you would ever get it. Monaco is prosperous, but small. Her only asset is a negation – she has no fog! So the rich come from England, Germany and Russia, and spend their money here. In return we exercise discretion: discretion as to who they are with, and what they do.'

'I must try,' said Bragg.

'Of course.' Doriot spread his hands with a grimace. 'I am sorry, but I am unable to come with you.'

'Yes,' said the dapper young manager, poring over the cheque in front of him. 'Yes, this cheque has been drawn on an account at this branch.'

'And whose is the signature on it?'

'I cannot tell you that, beyond saying that it is a client of the bank.'

'I know that,' retorted Bragg irritably. 'Is it Charles Meyer?'

Watching keenly, Morton fancied a flicker of recognition crossed the manager's face.

'I cannot answer such a question.'

'Is it Charles Cross?'

'I cannot answer ...'

'When was payment of the cheque stopped?'

The manager shook his head slowly and emphatically. 'Without the written permission of the holder of this account, or an order from the magistrate, I cannot answer your questions. Perhaps,' he added with an ironic smile, 'you should go to see the police. Good day, gentlemen.'

'That's it, then,' said Bragg savagely as they walked

through the gardens towards the Casino. 'We might as well turn it in; the buggers have won, as usual.'

'I could have sworn he recognized Charles Meyer's name,' said Morton.

'You caught it too? Yes, I think there's something there, but our chances of getting at it are non-existent. I told you, lad, once they start they can sew it up as tight as a sheep's arsehole. When's the next train back home?'

'I doubt if we'd get a sleeper now,' remarked Morton. 'I think it would be better to stay here tonight, and start back first thing tomorrow.'

'All right,' said Bragg grumpily. 'Find me a cheap hotel I can justify to Forbes, and leave me to get on with my report.'

'The Hôtel des Princes looked just the thing,' suggested Morton. 'A fine view over the harbour! You won't mind if I stay elsewhere, will you? I fancy a turn or two at the tables. After all, I am supposed to be on leave.'

'You carry on, lad. Pick me up straight after breakfast. Now let's have a beer before we go for our luggage.'

Morton spent the rest of the afternoon in Monte Carlo, rediscovering its steep streets and stairways. He revelled in its self-confidence, was cheered at its exuberance, and amused by its baroque extravagances. He browsed around the shops, and bought a silk-covered engagement book for his mother, and a gold locket for Bella. As the assistant wrapped up the little boxes, he decided that when he got back to London he would have a new photograph taken, and put a copy in the locket before giving it to her. Then, slipping the boxes into the pocket of his ulster, he turned towards the Hôtel de Paris.

The reception clerk was occupied with a large German woman, who wanted to get some jewellery out of the safe. While he was waiting, Morton idly flipped through the register. Suddenly his eye was caught by an entry in a strong assertive hand:

Sir Charles Cross, 45 Queen St., London W.

He took the pen and hurriedly scratched the room number on his left wrist, then registered his own name as inconspicuously as he could.

In his room Morton pondered the discovery, wondering whether he should alert Bragg immediately. Cross had already been in Monte Carlo for two days, but that knowledge would hardly take them any further. He decided to leave Bragg to his report, and watch for Cross himself.

He dressed carefully in his dress coat and a black silk sash, then had a solitary dinner in the corner of the marbled dining room, waiting for Sir Charles to appear. He sat long over his coffee and cognac, until the waiters began ostentatiously to clear the tables around him, then he strolled down to the gardens behind the Casino.

Across the harbour, the moon turned the battlements of Monaco into a fairy-tale castle. Below him a steamer was a Christmas-tree of lights, as it nosed gently in. The wind had dropped, and the mild air carried a faint scent of pine trees. In London it would be foggy, or snowy, or damp – all of them equally unpleasant. In a week or so scores of his acquaintances would be down here, transferring the location of their interminable parties in the search for a good time. Perhaps there was something to be said for it. He sighed with irritation at his own contrariness.

Following a winding path, he found himself at the front of the Casino, its high-baroque architecture softened in the moonlight. He went up the steps, and wandered slowly through the ornate salons with their marble pillars and painted panels. Already the rooms were crowded, the men attired in anything from dress coat to lounge suit. He excused himself from an attractive young lady in a feathered cap and *décolleté* dress who invited him to teach her how to play *vingt-et-un*, strolled past the black-jack tables and Americans shooting craps, and, paying the special membership fee, gained the room set aside for the serious gamblers. There was baccarat along one side, and in the centre, roulette tables. A crowd had gathered round one of them, and as Morton approached he could hear the deep voice of Sir Charles Cross raised in badinage with his party. One of the women was tipsy, and was upbraiding him for not increasing his stakes. Cross was expatiating on the subject of never selling when the market was dropping.

The crowd began to disperse, and Morton withdrew. Perhaps he could remember how to play *vingt-et-un* after all!

15

'Seven forty-eight is what we want!' cried Morton as he bounced into Bragg's room.

Bragg was shaving at the washing stand, his braces looping down and the neck of his woollen vest turned in. 'Oh hell! Have we missed it?' he asked, scowling at his reflecting in the speckled mirror.

'Not the train . . . the room!'

'Whatever are you on about?'

'Look, you can see the remains of it on my wrist: seven forty-eight. That's the number of Sir Charles Cross's room in the Hôtel de Paris.'

'In Monte Carlo?' asked Bragg in surprise.

'Yes. He's been here for a couple of days. I saw him last night in the Casino.'

'Did you now? How did he seem?'

'He sounded in a high good humour. Losing steadily, I should say, but not staking a lot.'

Bragg sluiced water from the bowl over his face, and rubbed it vigorously with a towel. Then he moved to the window and gazed thoughtfully across the harbour to Monaco. 'What time is it, lad?' he demanded.

'Just gone half past eight.'

'Time for a spot of breakfast, he remarked genially, 'and then we might see if our friend Doriot can be persuaded to change his mind.'

'You say the murderer is here in Monte Carlo?' Doriot seemed profoundly dejected by the news.

'Yes,' said Bragg, 'he's staying at the Hôtel de Paris.'

'I suppose you will be asking me to arrest him?' remarked Doriot with a grimace.

Bragg and Morton exchanged enquiring glances, then Bragg shook his head. 'No, not yet. The extradition proceedings are not complete.'

'Ah, I see,' said Doriot, brightening. 'How long will that take?'

'Today,' lied Bragg. 'I shall telegraph that he's here as soon as we get back from the bank.'

'Did you not go to the bank yesterday?'

'Yes, we did, and it was just as you said it would be. But now we are going back again to see if he'll change his mind – you too!'

'I cannot!' Doriot raised his hands to ward off this calamity. 'I told you the circumstances under which I work.'

'The circumstances have changed now,' said Bragg roughly. 'Cross is here in Monte Carlo, and we've got to do our damnedest to get him arrested before he leaves.'

'I can do nothing . . .'

'Yes, you can,' interrupted Bragg. 'You can squeeze that bank manager till he gives us some answers.'

'It is impossible!' cried Doriot in consternation.

'Look,' said Bragg, adopting a placatory tone. 'You have in Monte Carlo an international fraudsman and murderer, wanted by the English police and the French police alike. All I'm asking is that you help us to secure a crucial bit of evidence.'

Doriot shrugged unhappily, and said nothing.

'I know you're not trying to obstruct us, sir,' resumed Bragg reasonably, 'but it might look like that in London and Paris . . . and I know the Sûreté already regards Monaco as something of a fraudsmen's sanctuary.'

There was a pause, then Doriot raised disconsolate eyes to Bragg's face. 'It would appear that I have little choice,' he said plaintively.

'Good!' Bragg leapt to his feet and clapped Doriot on the shoulder. 'I have a cab outside. We asked him to wait.'

The manager had just arrived, and was still hanging up his coat when they were shown into his room. Bragg took a seat uninvited, and Morton and Doriot found chairs on either side of him. The manager was evidently unsettled by this discourtesy, for he began to walk to and fro behind his desk.

'I heard your questions yesterday.' he said irritably. 'Why have you come again?'

'Circumstances have changed, as the Inspector will tell you,' replied Bragg quietly, 'and it is important that we have answers.'

'How have they changed, Inspector?' demanded the manager.

Doriot smoothed his drooping moustache with the tips of his fingers. 'I cannot tell you how they have changed, m'sieur,' he said dolefully, 'but I must ask you to accept my assurances that they have changed.'

'But you are expecting me to answer these questions voluntarily? – without an order from the magistrate?' protested the manager indignantly.

'I would esteem it a personal favour, m'sieur,' said Doriot.

The manager stepped to the window, and gazed out over the boulevard. Then he turned, and sat down decisively at his desk. 'My reply to your questions, m'sieur, is this,' he said. 'There is no account open at this branch in the name of Charles Meyer or Sir Charles Cross.'

Incensed by this reverse, Bragg determined to stay on in Monte Carlo, and follow Cross when he left. He detailed Morton to watch the station, while he patrolled around the hotel. As he slowly paced the length of the Casino, across the terrace of the Café de Paris and round to the towering front of the hotel, Bragg became increasingly irked by the hobble that Sir William had put on him. Cross must realize they would check on the Meyer account. It seemed pointless to pretend Cross wasn't a suspect. What was he supposed to do if they met face to face? Say he was on holiday, and wish him good morning? If Cross left the hotel, perhaps he could contrive an encounter. There would be some questions then all right! Not that Sir William had actually forbidden questions, he'd just prohibited any kind of allegation. That seemed to give Bragg an opening he could exploit if he got the chance. Should Cross leave the hotel, he would force a meeting on him.

After a few more fruitless rounds in the chilly air, Bragg decided to storm the citadel. He mounted the steps, and, avoiding the enquiring eye of the porter, took the lift to the top floor. He followed a long carpeted corridor, which brought him to the seaward side of the hotel. He rapped on the door of room 748, and heard a shout from within. A moment later the door was flung open, and Cross greeted him confidently.

'Sergeant Bragg!' he exclaimed with a warm smile. 'I thought it was an official knock. Come in, I've been expecting you. Do sit down. Will you have a little something to keep out the cold?'

'No thank you, sir.'

'Very well. I gather from Maître Rochat that you've found out about the Meyer account. A harmless subterfuge, I assure you.'

'You knew about it all along, sir?' asked Bragg guardedly.

'Yes, I'm afraid I deceived you there,' smiled Cross apologetically. 'But as I knew it was all above board, I couldn't see how it would hinder your enquiries.'

'Why did you set it up, sir?'

'I wanted to create a fund overseas. It's always useful to have a reserve for contingencies – especially if the tax people don't know about it,' he added with a twinkle.

'I understand the business is owned by a company now.'

'Yes,' admitted Cross, startled.

'And that a substantial shareholding is held by a bank.'

'True, sergeant, but I fail to see the significance of that. I'm still the major shareholder.'

'Was the bank aware of the Meyer account, sir?'

'Ah,' said Cross with a relieved smile. 'I get your drift. No, this was in the nature of a concealed reserve – perfectly normal in shipping, as you must know.'

'Has the bank any representatives on the board of Cross Shipping, sir?' enquired Bragg, doggedly.

'Yes, John Turnbull is a director.'

'To look after the bank's interests?'

'If you like.'

'And did you tell him about it?'

'Good heavens, no, sergeant! He wouldn't have wanted to know, it would have embarrassed him. A banker is the last person to enquire about concealed reserves. They have millions stacked away their shareholders don't know about – and all with the Government's blessing.'

'And what happened to the Meyer cheques when they left the lawyer in Lyon?'

'They didn't leave him. He paid them into a joint bank account in his own name and that of Cross Shipping.'

'Would you give me a letter authorizing Rochat to disclose details of the account to me, sir?'

'That's hardly necessary,' replied Cross coldly. 'It's all there, you can take my word.'

'Does Cross Shipping or Charles Meyer have a bank account in Monte Carlo?' asked Bragg evenly.

'No. Why?'

'Your Mr Potter received a large cheque from someone, drawn on the Crédit Lyonnais in Monte Carlo.'

'Really?' exclaimed Cross. 'Sounds very odd.'

'I wonder if there might be some connection with his work.'

'We don't deal with anyone in Monte Carlo,' mused Cross, 'or with anyone operating here to my knowledge. You can see what kind of place it is.'

'Have you any notion where he might have got the cheque from, sir?'

'Sorry, sergeant, I can't help you on that.'

'You've no idea who could have killed Potter?'

'As I told you before, it must have been an accident or something entirely unconnected with us. And now, sergeant,' he went on with an affable smile, 'I hope I can be allowed to continue my holiday in peace. To save you patrolling about in the cold, I can tell you that tonight I shall be going to hear Vergnet sing *Faust*, and after that I may play a little roulette.'

Having hung around the station for a couple hours, Morton was beginning to be an object of considerabe interest to the white-gloved policeman who strolled by every quarter hour. After Constable Evans in Islington, Morton was wary of professional interest, and decided to come to the station only for the twenty minutes before a train was due. The intervening time he spent wandering around the neighbouring streets, gazing into the shops, and keeping a discreet eye on the traffic. In a jeweller's window he noticed a locket that was much more attractive than the one he had bought for Bella. He lifted his head, wondering whether to buy it, and there she was, trotting down the hill in a victoria . . . at least it looked like her . . . 'Bella! Bella!' he shouted, racing down the road after her. 'Bella!'

The golden head turned, and a face peeped over the back, then the carriage pulled to the side of the road and stopped.

'Bella! I thought it was you,' he gasped.

'James! How lovely to see you! What are you doing here?' she asked, her eyes sparkling.

'I . . . er . . . I've got some clients here.'

'Jump in!' she patted the seat beside her. 'I'm just going down to the port, so you can come with me.'

'The port?'

'Yes, I arrived by train yesterday, and my things went on board this morning. I've been seeing the sights, and I'm to be at the quay at noon.'

'I wish I'd known you were in Monte Carlo last night.'

'Now, naughty!'

'What's all this going on board business?'

'Didn't I tell you?' she asked airily. 'Oh no, I haven't seen you since. It all happened so quickly! My gentleman friend is taking me on a cruise with him.'

'A cruise?' echoed Morton, his heart sinking.

'Yes. We're stopping at Port Said, Aden, Mombassa,

Madagascar and Cape Town.' She told them off on her fingers, her face glowing with excitement.

'When are you coming back?' he asked dully.

'I don't know. He says we may never come back. But he's only teasing.'

'Oh no!' cried Morton.

'Now don't be silly! Of course we'll come back, and I'll look you up the moment I get to London.'

'You needn't bother,' exclaimed Morton.

'Now don't be a silly boy,' she pouted. 'You know I love you best. Come on, smile for me!'

Morton felt the sudden urge to protest his own affection, and to tell her she was going away with a cheat and murderer. But looking at her pert, shining face, he knew it wouldn't make any difference. He twisted his face into a grimace.

'That's better,' she smiled. 'Now you must get out here, we mustn't be seen together.'

'I bought you a present,' he said dolefully, plunging his hand into his coat pocket. 'I suppose it will be a goodbye present now.'

Bella looked solemn. 'Oh, James,' she breathed, hugging the little box to her bosom. 'I shall open it tonight, when I'm quite alone.' She turned her face appealingly towards him. 'Kiss me, James.'

He bent forward and kissed her briefly on the cheek. 'Goodbye, Bella.'

'Goodbye, James,' she said tenderly. Don't forget – the minute I get back!'

Bragg got back to his room to find Morton sprawled on the bed.

'What's up with you?' he asked. 'You look like a mute at an undertaker's funeral!'

'I've just seen Bella,' muttered Morton.

'Where?'

'Down by the harbour. She was just going on board

Cross's yacht. See,' he motioned Bragg to the window. 'That big white steamer lying well out.'

'That's the *Athena*, is it? remarked Bragg.

'I saw the thing come in last night,' said Morton morosely. 'Thought how beautiful it looked.'

'Did you speak to her?' asked Bragg gently.

'Yes, she's going on a cruise with him. "Port Said, Aden, Mombassa",' he mimicked, ' "Madagascar, Cape Town . . . We may never come back." Silly bitch! I even gave her a farewell present!' he cried in mortification. 'Though, trust me, I got that wrong as well. Instead of giving her the box with the locket, I gave her mother's engagement book by mistake.'

'Keep your locket for your next lady-love,' advised Bragg gruffly. 'As for Bella, a girl like her should find an engagement book very useful – keep all her men apart!'

Morton looked bleakly at the *Athena* riding at her anchor.

'That's very interesting, what Bella told you about going to Cape Town and never coming back,' said Bragg. 'Cross just assured me everything was above board. "Just a harmless subterfuge, sergeant". Patronizing bugger! But that doesn't chime with upping sticks to the Cape . . . He said Rochat banked all the Meyer cheques in Lyon, but he wouldn't let me question him about the account . . . Cracks on he can't understand how Potter came to get a cheque from Monte Carlo . . . And I don't believe a sodding word he says! Come on, lad, stop being sorry for yourself, we're going to ask Sir William to start extradition proceedings. We've got to compose a telegram even they can't wriggle out of!'

16

'Glorious, isn't it!' exclaimed Morton, his head full of the rich sonorities and soaring melodies. 'And I've never heard *Faust* sung better.'

They were strolling round the edge of the Casino's foyer, Bragg drawing self-consciously on a cigar in honour of his dress coat, but seeming to get little satisfaction from it.

'I'm glad you're enjoying it, lad,' he said grudgingly. 'To a heathen like me it's a penance. Give me Vesta Tilly any time.'

They cut inwards to avoid a group of chattering, bejewelled ladies and their escorts.

'Why, damn it,' he went on, 'we shall have heard this thing twice before we're finished! They encored the soldier, and that Mephistopheles song in the second act, and in this last one we had the bit where she was putting on the jewels three times! Three times! I ask you!'

'But surely you have encores at the Empire?'

'Course we do. That's different. This is supposed to be a serious story. You shouldn't keep stopping and shouting "Let's have that bit again", it makes it like a pantomime!'

He scowled at the end of his cigar, which had gone out, and stuffed it in his pocket. 'Mind you,' he continued, 'that trick with the inn sign was every bit as good as Drury Lane. I wonder how they managed it.'

'There must be two taps on the barrel. They turn the wine off and the gas on at the same moment, so that it looks as if the wine has turned to flame.'

'Must be something like that, with a little pilot light . . . Be a laugh if it blew out! Come on, we'd better go in for the second half of our sentence. Where's our man?'

'I saw him go into the bar when we came out. I expect he's

back inside now. Come to think of it, *Faust* is somehow very appropriate for Cross.'

They resumed their seats in the scarlet and gold Salle Garnier as the house lights dimmed. Bragg peered towards the front, where Cross's party was, but people were standing in the way.

'What are we in for now?' he asked.

'The church scene.'

'Oh my God!' muttered Bragg.

The orchestra began, the audience settled and the curtains parted. The light from the stage was dim, but Bragg thought he could detect a gap where Cross's head had been.

'Can you see him?' he whispered to Morton.

'What?' asked Morton, half lost in the music.

'I think he's gone!'

Morton stood to get a better view, ignoring the protests from behind. 'He's not there!' he hissed.

Bragg burst along the row, brushing unceremoniously past outraged patrons, and flung through the door into the foyer. 'You watch the front,' he called over his shoulder, 'and follow him if you see him. I'm going in after him!'

He raced across the road and bounded up the stairs in the domed hall of the hotel. There was a crowd waiting for the lift, and he lost precious seconds casting about for the staircase. When he reached the top he was short of breath and his heart was pounding. He was only halfway down the corridor when he saw a door open, and Cross come out. He had changed from his dress suit and was wearing a heavy travelling coat. In his hand he held a Gladstone bag. Cross locked the door, and at Bragg's approach, looked up. At first he affected not to recognize him, and made to brush past, but Bragg barred his way.

'What the devil is this?' Cross demanded furiously.

'I want to talk to you,' gasped Bragg, bracing himself for an attack.

'More questions?'

'No, I'm going to give you the answers.'

Cross's body tensed for a spring, and then relaxed as

women's voices were heard down the corridor. 'Very well,' he said angrily. 'But not in the corridor, we'll go in here.'

He opened a door, and led Bragg on to a little pillared terrace with one side open to the sky. The tea-tables of summer were pushed together against the low balustrade, and brooms and buckets were piled in a corner.

Cross placed his bag on one of the tables, and took a chair. 'Since we must talk,' he remarked with forced bonhomie, 'we might as well be comfortable. Do sit down, sergeant, I promise to hear you out.'

Bragg felt with irritation that the initiative was slipping away from him. 'You told me a lot of nonsense this morning,' he said, 'and now I'm going to tell you what really happened.'

'So be it.' Cross unbuttoned his coat and took a cigar case from his pocket. 'Will you?' he asked, offering it to Bragg.

Bragg shook his head.

'You don't mind if I do? . . . Good.' He slid the band off his cigar and produced a gold cutter from his waistcoat. 'Please proceed, sergeant.'

It was like giving evidence at the Lord Mayor's court, thought Bragg. 'You set the Meyer account up when you sold the shares to the bank,' he began. 'You told me it was a business reserve, but it wasn't. You always intended that money for yourself.'

Cross regarded Bragg judicially, the smoke from his cigar curling up in the light air.

'You told me the Meyer cheques were banked in Lyon, but they weren't. Rochat sent them to the account in Monte Carlo that you closed a couple of days ago.'

Cross shook his head gently.

'Then Potter tumbled to what was happening, I don't know how, and began blackmailing you. In November you bought him off with a cheque from the Meyer account, and then murdered him. You destroyed the records you knew about, and made out he had been killed by footpads.'

'These are absurd allegations,' said Cross, inspecting the

end of his cigar. 'At the time Potter died I was at home. You can easily verify it.'

'Oh, you didn't do it yourself, you paid some heavies from Millwall to do it for you.'

'You can prove that?'

'We shall.'

Cross brushed ash off his coat sleeve, and looked over his shoulder towards the harbour. 'I think I should put you right on Potter,' he said.

'Then I must warn you that your words will . . . ' began Bragg.

'Yes, yes. I know all about that,' interrupted Cross irritably. 'I'm not going to tell you anything the slightest bit criminal.' He paused, and assumed a casual tone. 'You are right about the Meyer account,' he said. 'As I've explained, it was a genuine business reserve, but it had to be cloaked in this way, otherwise the transaction it was intended for would have been imperilled.'

'What was that?' asked Bragg, but Cross waved aside the question.

'Potter discovered the arrangements, entirely by accident. One of the steam-and-sail ships met unexpectedly strong winds in the Bay of Biscay, and her captain was forced to use the engine. He called at Gibraltar to top up his bunkers for the trip to Mombassa. Of course, Potter received the invoice for this, and, in addition, one showing that it had also refuelled at Marseilles. He jumped to the conclusion that something underhand was going on, and came to see me. He threatened to reveal what he had found to the police and the bank. Naturally, I wasn't concerned about the police,' he went on with a smile, 'but it would have been inconvenient for me if the bank had known at that time. I was negotiating to buy a company they had an interest in, and had they got to know, it might have proved difficult. So I bought Potter off for fifty pounds, to give me time to close the deal. But he was greedy as well as criminal, and, just as the documents were at the final draft stage, he came again and demanded a very large sum. It was a preposterous position. I was being subjected to blackmail over an innocent commercial transaction – but I had to keep it secret for a few more days. I wrote him a cheque on the Monte Carlo account to satisfy him.'

'And then?' prompted Bragg.

'Since there was no substance to his allegations, I saw no reason to honour the cheque. I asked the manager of the docks office to get the cheque off him, and to persuade him not to be so stupid in future. I was horrified to hear that he was dead, but I am satisfied there was no connection between the attack and my instructions.'

'And what about the purchase of the company, sir?' asked Bragg.

'Oh, it went through a couple of days later.'

'Then the money won't be in this bag at all?' As he spoke, Bragg flung himself at the Gladstone bag, and wrapped his arms round it.

Cross seized the handles, and tried to tear it away. They struggled over the bag, kicking and butting, neither prepared to relax his hold. Then Bragg twisted sideways and managed to get it under his arm. With the other hand he began to prise Cross's fingers from one handle. Cross dropped his head, and bit Bragg savagely across the knuckles. Bragg thrust him hard against a pillar, and with a final twist wrested one handle away from him. But now Cross held the other with both hands. He braced his foot against the pillar and, leaning outwards, gave a desperate heave. There was a ripping sound, and the handle came away. Cross was catapulted backwards on to the tables, his body slid over the smooth marble, and with a scream he disappeared over the balustrade.

Bragg raced down the stairs, and round the side of the hotel. A crowd was beginning to collect in the dim light, and Morton was kneeling by the crumpled body.

'What happened?' he asked.

'I don't know,' replied Bragg. 'I just heard a scream. Is he dead?'

'Smashed to pieces . . . Poor Bella!'

'Go and get a policeman!' snapped Bragg. 'And ask these people to stand back.'

He gazed down at the shattered body, then stooped and, opening the clenched fingers, took the handle and put it in his pocket.

The waterman shipped his oars, and the boat grated against the *Athena*'s side. As Morton made his way up the accommodation ladder, he was aware of an officer standing at its head. 'Take me to the captain, please,' he said.

'Who are you?' asked the officer aggressively.

'Never mind that – the captain, and quickly!'

The man hesitated, then, jerking his head for Morton to follow, led him to the chart room. The captain was leaning over a large table, with a chart of the eastern Mediterranean on it. As Morton entered, he straightened up and threw his dividers on the table. 'Yes?' he asked.

'My name is Morton. I am a British police officer.'

The captain examined the identity card with surprise.

'I'm afraid I have to tell you,' went on Morton, 'that your employer is dead.'

'Dead?'

'Yes. He fell from the top floor of the Hôtel de Paris this evening, and was killed.'

'God Almighty!' The captain subsided into his chair. 'It's unbelievable! Was it an accident?'

'It must have been. He was on a little open-air terrace. They think he must have tripped and gone over the balustrade.'

'You're not having me on the stick, are you?' asked the captain, then dropped his eyes to Morton's card. 'No, I can see you're not.'

'The Monaco authorities will want the body for a couple of days, then it can be taken back to England. Will you take it on board when it's released?'

'It's a week's voyage,' objected the captain. 'He might not keep all that well. I might have to bury him at sea, and the family wouldn't like that.'

'Then he'd better go back on the train. Will you see to it?'

'Yes. I'll get our agents to arrange everything ... We might as well weigh anchor tonight, we've got steam up. That is if he really is dead.'

'You'd better go to the mortuary, if you still don't believe me. Now, I'd like to have a word with Miss Berkeley.'

The captain raised his eyebrows in momentary surprise. 'Yes, of course. I'll take you to her.'

Morton followed him down the companionway to a cabin on the next deck, where he rapped on the door.

'Miss Berkeley,' he called, 'a gentlemen to see you!'

'Come in! I'm decent!' gurgled Bella happily. As Morton crossed the threshold her smile faded. 'James! What are you doing here? ... I told you not to pester me. You'll spoil everything!'

'I'm sorry if you were expecting Sir Charles,' said Morton coolly. 'I'm afraid there's nothing to spoil. I've come to take you home. Sir Charles is dead.'

'You can't cod me like that,' retorted Bella angrily. 'I'm not coming anywhere with you. I'm going to Cape Town, and you're not stopping me!'

'I tell you Sir Charles Cross is dead!'

'I don't believe you! You've never liked me being friends with him. You'd have done anything to stop me coming if you'd known!'

'The captain is going to the mortuary,' said Morton in a level voice, 'then he's going to weigh anchor for England. If you want to come back by train, you'd better leave the ship now.'

'But he can't be dead!' cried Bella wildly. 'He was here this morning, and he was perfectly well then.'

'He fell from the top of the hotel, and was killed instantly.'

'How do you know?'

'I was walking by at the time, and I found him.'

'If he fell, it was because you pushed him!' shouted Bella. 'I know what happened! You just want me for yourself!'

'Bella!' Morton crossed the cabin, and took her elbow.

'You're talking wildly. I had no reason to wish Sir Charles Cross dead.'

'Yes, you had!' cried Bella. 'How is it that you know his name, anyway? I never told you!'

Morton hesitated. 'He was one of my clients.'

'I don't believe you. He could have seen you in London, you wouldn't need to come down here.'

'Very well, I suppose you deserve to know the truth. Sir Charles Cross was a fraudsman, and probably a murderer into the bargain. I am a policeman . . . '

'Policeman!' she cried, wrenching her arm away. 'So that's the truth of it. It was him you wanted, not me! All the time we were together, you were pretending.'

'Bella, I swear that's not true,' retorted Morton in irritation.

'Yes, you were! You'd always bring the conversation round to him. I thought you were jealous. What a fool I was!'

'Come back to London, I'll look after you.'

'Not now, you won't. I've finished with you. Spying, creeping swine you are!'

'Bella,' urged Morton, 'come back with me, and get away from this horrible business.'

'You hounded him!' screamed Bella. 'If he's dead, you murdered him! Get out! Get out!' She flung herself on the bed in hysterical rage.

'You know where I live, if you need me,' said Morton angrily, and banged out of the cabin.

Morton stared moodily out of the window as the train made for Marseilles. Most of the time they were in cuttings, but occasionally he glimpsed the leaden sea probing into the blood-red rocks of the coves. He was angry with Bella, mortified too with himself. How ludicrous to get into a brawl because she preferred Cross to him. Bragg had been right about getting involved – as usual. Still it was a pity . . . She'd certainly been something special in bed . . . He followed his usual practice at this stage of an affair, and tried to imagine her at The Priory: at table in the great hall, in the drawing-room, in his parents' bedroom; trying to project her image on to the backdrop of Ashwell. She failed the test – of course she did. What a fool he was!

With the fading light they pulled out of St Raphael and swung inland. Morton looked across at Bragg, pencilling notes for his report. 'Not a very successful case, was it?' he observed grumpily.

'I suppose that depends on how you see it.' answered Bragg, puffing contentedly at his pipe. 'We aren't bringing him back in handcuffs to face the full panoply of the law, but that apart things have turned out quite well.'

'I don't see how you can say that,' objected Morton. 'His crimes will never be made public, in people's eyes he will still be a respectable City figure. That can't be right.'

'Publicity's a tricky thing, lad. One thing's for sure, it wouldn't hurt Cross, only those he's left behind.'

'It would have discouraged other people from doing the same.'

'Aye, there is that – if we'd got a conviction.'

'But surely there's no doubt about it?' protested Morton.

'There's always doubt until you've got the jury's verdict. We know he had Potter murdered, but a good counsel would have made out he'd nothing to do with the attack. He might even have got off – especially if the prosecution weren't trying.'

'Surely that's unthinkable?'

'Why is it? The City of London is supposed to be ruled by men of honesty and integrity, that's why it's the trading capital of the world. No government would welcome some stupid copper proving that's all moonshine! All you need is for the Attorney General to lead for the prosecution, and tip him the wink not to win.'

'But if the evidence is there, a conviction must follow.'

'The evidence has to be led,' replied Bragg, stabbing the air emphatically with his pipe stem. 'The witnesses have to be questioned, the documents have to be explained. When you've seen as many cases bungled as I have, you'll begin to have your doubts too. Cross didn't pay the penalty according to the law, but he's dead. Anyone looking fairly at the evidence will be convinced he was guilty. What more do you want? Let's go for some dinner, I'm hungry.'

Bragg seized the menu with zest. 'Tomorrow, it'll be back to steak pie and roly-poly,' he laughed. 'I must say the French do themselves very well for food. What's this?' he asked of a passing waiter.

'Diable de mer, sir? Eet is how you say in Engleesh, zee angler feesh – very good.'

Bragg grimaced at Morton as the waiter turned away. 'They eat some damned funny things, mind you. I've seen one of those at Billingsgate, ugly-looking devils with jaws like a man-trap. Next time Mrs Jenks asks me what I'd like for dinner, I'll say "Diable de mer en papillote, sauce béarnaise". That'll fix her!' He chuckled. 'Ah, he wants our order; better concentrate ... Have you got any of those grenouilles things I had coming down?' he asked. 'They were very tasty.'

'The frogs' legs? Yes, sir.'

'Frogs? ... Oh Christ! ... You rotten bugger!'

Epilogue

'I've read your report, Bragg,' said Sir William, warming his back at the fire. 'Funny business. You wouldn't think someone in his position would stoop to fraud, would you?'

'When people are used to money,' replied Bragg, 'it's often intolerable for them to be without it.'

'What? Oh, yes. And the money proved it, of course. Lucky you found that old bag when his room was searched. I suppose there's no doubt it was the same money?'

'None at all. The bank confirmed that they were the notes Cross had drawn out on the fifth. I gather there was only one bundle not accounted for.'

'And he admitted giving the cheque to Potter?'

'Yes. sir. He stopped payment of it as soon as he'd written it.'

'I suppose we couldn't have got him for murder?' wondered Sir William.

'Not unless one of the gang gave evidence against him. But it was manslaughter on his own admission.'

'Saved us a lot of trouble, his committing suicide. Mind you, I'm surprised. I wouldn't have thought he was the type.'

'He must have realized that wherever he went, you'd have an extradition warrant waiting for him.'

'It's a good thing for his family the French brought it off as an accident. Still, it must have been a terrible shock for his poor wife. How is she fixed? Do you know?'

'I imagine the bank will buy her out – she'll manage,' said Bragg shortly.

'That's all right then. Well, we were lucky to get out of it with so little fuss. In some ways it was better than a full-scale trial. That wouldn't have gone down well in the City.

You'd be surprised, Bragg, how sensitive it is to the least breath of scandal. Even charging Cross with fraud would have brought the stockmarket down ten points.'

'Yes, sir.'

'Right, you can go now . . . and well done!' Sir William held out a grudging hand, and Bragg took it.

'See you've hurt your hand, Bragg.'

'Caught it in the train door, sir.'

Bragg thrust the hand into his pocket, and a faint smile came to his lips as his fingers touched the thick bundle of franc notes. They would help Daisy Potter to manage, as well!